SEQUESTERED WITH MY STEPBROTHER

SUBMITTING TO MY STEPBROTHER
BOOK THREE

M. FRANCIS HASTINGS

For my mom who swears she'll never read my smut.

CONTENTS

TRAPPED IN SUBURBIA

-Jacey-

"Oh my dear! Are you all right?!" Petra asked, scurrying over to me. "Roy, get something to clean this up!"

I stared at Leon, who grinned at me. I didn't like the look of his grin.

Caleb put his arm around me, a fake smile plastered on his face. I knew it was a fake smile because I knew all his smiles. I also knew he'd heard what Leon said and come to the same conclusion.

I decided I needed to up my game, too. My smile shook, but I managed to put one on my face. "I'm sorry, Petra. It slipped right out of my hand."

"Condensation," Caleb added.

"Of course, my dear," Petra said sympathetically. "Roy!"

Roy hurried over with a broom and dustpan. Once the glass was cleaned up, he came over with the hose to just wash whatever was left into the lawn. "Petra, get Ange another glass. Can't have her dehydrating in her condition."

"No, we can't." Gail quite rudely rubbed my belly.

"Please don't do that without asking." Caleb defended me.

I clutched the edge of his shirt, using my hold on him to ground myself.

Petra came over with another glass and patted Jacey on the back. "Drink up, dear. And don't worry about the glass. I've always hated that set."

"Hey! My mother gave those to us!" Roy protested.

"All the more reason to hate it," Petra muttered and gave us a wink.

Caleb went back to cutting my steak, but I knew he was eyeing Leon and Gail. Were we in danger? Should we call Darren?

We'd been very fortunate in the fact that Darren had taken over overseeing our witness protection arrangements himself, not trusting anyone else to do it.

"Mark, do you think you should make that call?" I whispered. "The one to Dad? He's not feeling very well."

Caleb nodded and stood, pulling a cell phone out of his pocket. "I'm sorry, will you excuse me a moment?"

"I think you should call your dad later," Leon smiled, but there was a significant look in his eyes. "Pretty sure he's not home right now on a lovely day like this."

"Pretty sure he won't be home for a while," Gail murmured when Roy and Petra began bickering over the fruit salad.

Oh God. Had something happened to Darren?!

Caleb's eyes slid to Roy and Petra. Satisfied they weren't listening, he speared Leon with a glare. "What do you want?"

"Just to see the little bundle of joy is being well taken care of." Gail trilled a laugh. But her eyes were hard, dead.

I wondered if these were hired mercenaries. Whatever they were, they felt dangerous.

Caleb must have felt the same way because his arm around me tightened. "The bundle of joy isn't due for another two months. But he's doing just fine, thank you."

"Oh, we know. We've been keeping track," Leon said.

I let out a low whimper, and Caleb went white with rage. "If you don't leave us alone, it could hurt the baby," he hissed.

"Mr. Masterson thought it was about time you came home. I hope you enjoyed your vacation," Gail smirked.

"Where's Darren?" I blurted.

"Who's Darren?" Petra asked.

None of us had even realized the Hendersons had finished fighting.

"A mutual friend we just realized we have. Back in Minnesota," Leon said easily.

"He's been sick lately," Gail lamented. "Laid up in the hospital, poor thing. He had a terrible accident. He might have even suffered a brain injury." She looked at Caleb. "It's so horrible when bad things happen to good friends."

Leon was eyeing the Hendersons speculatively.

I dug my nails into Caleb's thigh.

"It is horrible. Luckily, it doesn't happen that often. In fact, I don't think it'll happen again for a long time," Caleb said.

"No. Not for a long time. But you really should go visit Darren. We can make all the arrangements. We wouldn't want to put any more stress on poor Angela here than we already have," Gail replied, examining her nails.

"Oh, you need to go to Minnesota to visit your friend?" Petra asked.

Roy was frowning now. I think he was getting the idea that something was amiss.

Please don't say anything. Please don't say anything, I silently begged, hoping either Roy or God could hear me.

"Hey, is something going on here? You're looking pretty squirrely, Mark. Are you guys upsetting Angela? She's pregnant, you know. If you're going to be doing upsetting things and having upsetting conversations, you can lea—" Roy began.

Leon pulled out a gun with a silencer on it and shot Roy in the forehead.

"No!" I screamed.

Caleb shot up to stop Leon, but Gail grabbed him by the shirt, and Leon quickly dispatched Petra as well.

"I wouldn't mess with Leon, Caleb," Gail said flatly.

To illustrate her point, Leon pointed his gun at Caleb.

I threw myself in front of him. "No, no!"

"We should get going," Gail added in a bored tone while Leon winked at us and put his gun back in an arm holster under his Hawaiian shirt. "I'm sure Jacey is quite upset now, and since we don't want her going into labor while we're in Arizona, time is of the essence."

"She shouldn't fly," Caleb said, sitting back down and embracing me. "Especially now that you've upset her."

"Too bad. We've already got the doctor's note. She's only seven months along. That's six weeks before they'd stop her from flying," Leon snorted. He grabbed me roughly by the arm.

I squeaked in pain.

Gail rolled her eyes. "I swear, Leon, you have the delicacy of an elephant." She swatted Leon's hand off me. "You, get her ready to go," she barked at Caleb.

Caleb glared at her but stood and helped me to my feet. He held me against him, rubbing his hands up and down my back. "It's going to be okay," he whispered in my ear. "Everything's going to be okay."

I hiccuped a sob but let Caleb comfort me. I knew as long as I had him, everything would be fine.

Gail and Leon quickly spirited us away in a black sedan from the Hendersons' house. I felt sick to my stomach over what had happened to them, and between the horror of it and pregnancy hormones, I couldn't stop crying.

At the airport, I got several strange looks. Caleb just held me and pasted on his fake smile. "Hormones," he said to those who asked. "What are you gonna do?"

Gail and Leon got us through the airport rather quickly and out to a private jet. I stumbled when I saw Mr. Masterson coming down the stairs to greet us, Will in his wake.

"Thought you could escape forever, did you?" Mr. Masterson asked pleasantly. Will just looked down at the tarmac. "Well, you were wrong about that, weren't you?"

"Yes, sir," I said quietly.

"What do you want, Masterson?" Caleb seethed.

Mr. Masterson raised an eyebrow. "Caleb, you're not that dense. You know what I want."

I put my hands protectively over my belly, and Caleb put a hand over mine.

"You're not getting my son," Caleb hissed.

"Oh, but it's Will's son. I made sure of that," Mr. Masterson chuckled. "And yes, I am getting him. His name will be William Masterson as well. Traditions are important, you see."

"So, in vitro fertilization on someone who doesn't want to be pregnant, an eighteen-year-old girl, no less, is somehow a tradition?" Caleb said, glowering at Mr. Masterson. "And how do you know she didn't miscarry, and we're having my son?"

"Caleb, Caleb, Caleb. You try so hard," Mr. Masterson tsked. "But you're just out of your league. She's a piss poor liar, and you're not much better."

Caleb held me close. "Leave us alone, Masterson."

"And you and I both know that won't be happening. Come on, now. Up on the plane you go." Mr. Masterson motioned for us to follow him onto the plane.

Will could barely look at us. He limped onto the plane as well.

"Oh God, what did Mr. Masterson do to him?" I gasped to Caleb as we followed our captor and my baby's father onto the plane.

"Nothing he won't get used to," Mr. Masterson said.

Gail and Leon followed us onto the plane and sat near us.

Will started to sit down by his father, but Mr. Masterson gave him a sharp look. "Tell your friends of your adventures, Will. Go on. Go sit by them."

With a wince, Will hobbled over to us. He sat down across from Caleb, his eyes on the floor.

"Will?" Caleb asked.

"Father had my legs broken." Will said softly. His eyes were swimming with tears when he looked up at us. "I won't be able to help you again."

I reached across the space between us and took his hand. "It's all right. You tried. I can't imagine what you've been through."

Will shivered. "It was worth it," he replied in a low tone. "Or at least it would have been if Father hadn't found you. Darren… Darren is in the ICU. He held out for so long."

A tear rolled down my cheek, and Caleb rubbed the back of my neck. "Is he going to be okay?"

"I don't think so," Will whispered.

I closed my eyes against the tears, but they still rolled hot down my cheeks.

"Jacey," Will said, looking stricken. "There's more."

"How much more can there be?" Caleb grunted, but I patted his thigh to tell him to let Will continue.

"Father's taken your father…" Will turned to Caleb. "… and your mother hostage. And… and the little one, too. Timothy."

"Our little brother?" I gasped.

"Is he healthy?" Caleb asked.

"Timothy's fine. Your parents are fine. They're just living at the mansion, like you will be," Will mumbled.

Caleb laughed mirthlessly. "One big happy family, then."

Will looked at me, then back at the ground. "We'll be having another after this one."

"I-I sort of guessed," I whispered.

"Great," Caleb said angrily. "That's just great."

"Father doesn't want to pay for in vitro again," Will went on.

I felt the blood drain from my face. "What?"

"Oh, that's not happening," Caleb insisted. "That's not happening at all."

"Do you want to live?" Will asked.

Caleb scowled, but finally nodded his head.

"Father said it wasn't necessary to keep you alive, but I've convinced him otherwise. I said you'd be good about it," Will said. "Please, please don't make a liar out of me. I don't want him to have you killed. And I sure as hell don't want you to end up like Darren."

"When do I have to start being 'good about it'?" Caleb inquired bitterly.

"After Jacey has our son," Will responded. "Father doesn't want anything to interfere with that."

"I'm sure he doesn't." Caleb put his arm possessively around me.

Will hung his head. "I'm sorry I failed."

"Hey." Caleb bumped Will's ankle with his boat shoe. "You did all you could. And so did Darren. Your dad's just a bigger prick than anyone realized."

Will smiled just a little at that. "I promise I'll be good to her," he vowed to Caleb. Then he blushed and turned to me. "I promise I'll be good to you."

"I know. You're a good guy, Will," I replied softly.

"I'm glad you think so. I don't feel like a good guy. In two months, I'm going to be putting my dick in my best friend's girl," Will said gloomily. "I don't know what my father's obsession is with you. I really don't."

"She's pretty, she's available, and no one will miss her if something happens to her," Mr. Masterson piped up.

"I'll miss her," Caleb growled.

"You are inconsequential. I think you'd better take a leaf out of Will's book. Keep your head down and shut up," Mr. Masterson advised.

Caleb's hands balled into fists, but I gripped his thigh before he could say anything. "Let's just try to get through this," I breathed in his ear. "Please, don't get yourself killed."

"Yeah," Will said. "Please don't get yourself killed."

BACK IN THE MANOR

-Caleb-

Jacey's nails dug into my thigh all the way back to the Mastersons' mansion. I think she was trying to keep me quiet. I didn't want her to have to face all this alone, so I stayed quiet. As much as I hated Masterson, I knew he wasn't lying. I was inconsequential at this point. They were keeping me around just to keep Jacey happy.

I imagined the same could be said for my mother, her father, and baby Timothy. Everyone was woven into a carefully crafted web to ensnare Jacey into doing whatever Masterson wanted.

Hopefully, Masterson wasn't going to revisit fucking Jacey himself.

The mansion was just the same as we had left it. The decor was still inviting. It still had a happy, alive feeling.

It was also festooned with cameras that Masterson used to keep track of us and watch us have sex. I could see one perched ever so inconspicuously just above the crown molding. It was white, so it blended in quite well, and one wouldn't have seen it if one wasn't looking for it.

"Home sweet home," Masterson said, clapping me on the back. "Gosh, doesn't this bring back memories?"

It sure did. I remembered spending three months in confinement while they got Jacey pregnant with Will's baby.

"You'll be staying in your old room. Please feel free to use the pool," Masterson went on. "Your mother and stepfather are wandering around here somewhere with Timothy, I'm sure."

"What story did you tell them?" I asked.

Masterson grinned. "I told them the truth. That you came asking for my help, and Will's children are the price."

"I'm sure that went over real well with Hank," I scoffed.

That just made Masterson's smile widen and take on a touch of evil. "Hank saw the light of day. He isn't walking anymore, though. I wasn't terribly impressed with his beating his own daughter. That and his asinine objections, well, a lesson needed to be learned."

Jacey's hand flew to her mouth. "Is Dad okay?"

"He's fine. He has a nurse and your stepmother. Let's just say his legs did not heal as well as Will's did," Masterson said.

I put an arm around Jacey as her breath caught. "I thought we were trying not to upset Jacey."

Masterson shrugged. "She was going to see him anyway. Might as well rip the bandaid off now."

"Father," Will appeared at Masterson's shoulder. "Let's just get Jacey resting, okay? She's had a really traumatizing day."

"Yes, you're right, Will." Masterson patted his son on the head.

Will didn't look as though he appreciated the belittling gesture, but he didn't say anything. Instead, he herded the two of us back to our room, as though we might have forgotten where it was.

He sat down on our bed with a long sigh. "This is such a shit show. I can't believe I ever thought my father was a good man."

"He had us all believing he was. He's a great liar," I replied. I helped Jacey sit down, then both Will and I got her lying down on her side with pillows piled up so she was comfortable.

"Father is a great liar," Will agreed.

"You don't call him Dad anymore, I noticed," I said.

Will shrugged. "I'm allowed my small rebellions."

"Are you going to be okay?" Jacey asked. "I saw you limping."

"I'll always limp. But I'm a lot better off than your father. I'm sorry," Will replied.

"I'd like to say he had it coming," I said. "But it sounds like it sucks worse than what we thought he deserved."

"It does. He might never walk again," Will mumbled.

Jacey took a shaky breath, and I rubbed her calf. "Is your father at least letting him try?" I asked.

"Oh yes. He likes to watch Hank struggle," Will said darkly.

"Sounds like him." I locked eyes with Jacey and mouthed an 'I'm sorry.'

"They'll have been told you're here." Will glanced at the door. "I'm sure they'll be showing up any time now."

As though on cue, my mother came rolling up with Hank, a baby carrier strapped to her front. A fuzzy little head poked up out of the carrier, but that was about all we could see of Timothy. His hair.

Hank looked cranky, sitting in his chair. "Eighteen and pregnant. I couldn't be more proud."

"Nice to see you again, too, wheels," I shot back. "It's not like it's her fault."

"Funny, seems to me all this bad shit started when she started fucking her brother," Hank snapped.

"I'm not her brother," I sighed at the same time Will corrected him. "Stepbrother."

"It's sick," Hank grunted. "At least you're not the father."

I stood, ready to punch him, but Will grabbed my arm.

"It's not worth it. And you'll upset Jacey," he said quietly.

I lowered my fist. Hank, the bastard, actually smirked at me.

"Hotheaded as ever." Hank looked up at my mother. "See what a bad influence he is?"

My mother blushed. "I didn't realize they'd start... you knowing... together when she turned eighteen. If I had, I never would have introduced him into the family."

"Love you, too, Mom," I sassed.

"If you loved me, you wouldn't have put your thing in your sister," my mother sniffled.

"STEPSISTER!!!" Will, Jacey, and I corrected together.

"Whatever. Mr. Masterson tells me we're stuck here until Jacey whores for you again, Will," Hank grumbled. "I'm not real keen on the idea, but I guess I shouldn't complain." He gestured to his legs.

"You'd think that would've made you shut the fuck up," I complained.

Hank curled his lip at me. "This is all your fault."

"Dad! That's not true. And will you please stop insulting Caleb and me?" Jacey asked, tears streaming down her cheeks.

Seeing Jacey cry broke a dam in me, and I surged at Hank, ready to beat him to death.

Luckily for him, Will grabbed me and wrestled me to the floor.

"Get out!" Will yelled.

"I'm not done—" Hank started.

"OUT!!!" Will repeated.

My mother, prudently, wheeled Hank out.

"I think all we ever see of our brother might be the fuzz on top of his head." I sighed.

Jacey looked miserable. "I thought maybe we'd reconcile or something. Being in the same circumstances and all."

"Your dad is a dick. And I say that knowing full well what my dad is," Will said. "If he doesn't want to make up, that's on him. He's missing out, though."

Jacey gave Will a watery smile. "Thanks, Will."

"Just telling the truth," Will shrugged. "Do you want to go float in the pool? I hear pregnant women like that sort of thing. I've been… um… Googling."

"That's very responsible of you," I responded. "Getting ready to be a dad?"

"As much as my father will let me, I suppose. He's not exactly proud of me right now," Will muttered.

"That's so sweet, Will," Jacey smiled.

"I've been Googling, too," I confided. "There's a lot to know."

Will's cheeks turned pink. "This is probably a very inappropriate question, but is it true women have a heightened sex drive during pregnancy?"

"Yes," Jacey answered while my jaw dropped at the boldness of his question. "But it goes down again. I guess for four to six weeks after having the baby you're really not ready to resume sex."

"Good. I'll tell my father that. It'll give us more time to figure out what to do," Will said.

"Will," I replied, grabbing him by the shoulders. "You're not seriously thinking of trying to get us out again. Look what happened last time!"

"There's a lot more people now to get out, too," Jacey pointed out.

Will shrugged. "I'm not planning on letting my father get away with all of this. I know it'll be harder now, but there has to be a way."

"If you do find a way, you're coming with us," I said firmly.

"I'll have to. He said the next time he'd kill me," Will responded. "And I believe him."

"I'd believe him, too." I started pacing the floor. "There's cameras everywhere. Oh fuck, did your dad add sound to this room?"

"Yeah, it has sound. But I'm not saying anything that will surprise my father," Will said. "I did tell him I wouldn't let him get away with this. He's just probably watching right now, laughing his ass off at my rebellion. Since he knows I can't actually do anything."

I shook my head. "Don't press your luck, Will. It might not be just you who gets in trouble."

Will inclined his head at that, acknowledging my point. "Let's get Jacey in the pool. Do you want me to leave while the two of you get dressed?"

"I have a swimsuit on under my sundress," Jacey confessed.

"Are there swim shorts in here for both of us?" I asked Will.

Will opened the armoire and got out two pairs.

Jacey covered her face with her hands while Will and I changed, not for my sake, but for Will's. Then we got Jacey out of bed, and I stripped her sundress over her head.

Beneath, she was wearing a striped bikini.

Will stared for a moment longer than I felt was strictly necessary but then dragged his eyes away. We all walked out to the pool together, me supporting Jacey with an arm around her waist.

Will found a couple of pool noodles, and we got Jacey happily floating in the water. We bobbed around her, chatting as happily as we could, given the circumstances.

Before long, my mother came out with baby Timothy still strapped to her chest. Hank was not with her.

"Why do you have to antagonize Hank, Caleb?" she sighed, sitting at the edge of the pool and dangling her legs in the water.

I raised an eyebrow. "Me antagonize him? I think it's the other way around."

"If you could just stop… you know-ing… with Jacey…" my mother pleaded.

"What, so she can 'you know' with me instead?" Will snorted.

"As far as I've heard from Mr. Masterson, that's the plan," my mother said. "He says you two are going to have another baby the old-fashioned way. I can only assume he means that you will be having sex."

"Maybe he just said that to bother Hank. Trust me, I'd be tempted, and I'm not as big a bastard as Mr. Masterson," I replied.

My mother shook her head. "I believe him. He's sick and twisted, but it's not as twisted as what you're doing with your sister."

"She's not my sister," I said exasperatedly.

"I'm married to her father. She's your sister," my mother insisted.

"Jeanie," Jacey finally added to the conversation, "I don't like that you keep calling us brother and sister. We were teenagers when you and Dad got married. We're not biologically related, and your wanting to play 'happy families' is not going to make us that way. Caleb and I fell in love. That's that."

"And you and Will?" my mother asked.

I looked at my mother as though she'd grown another head. "You think Jacey's supposed to fall in love with Will now?"

"She's having his baby. It would be convenient," my mother replied uncomfortably.

"Wow, you are certifiable," I murmured. "You are truly, truly insane."

"I'm just trying to present the best solutions for everyone," my mother said, frustrated. "Maybe if you listened to me for once, we wouldn't be in this situation."

"As I recall, it was Hank being a dick that had us leaving camp that day. Everything snowballed from there. But you wouldn't blame your precious Hank for a damn thing, would you? Glad to know how I rank," I responded sarcastically.

My mother stood. "This is a really unproductive conversation. I'm going to go spend time with your father."

"Hank is not my father," I repeated for what must have been the thousandth time.

"And that must be why you think it's appropriate to screw his daughter," my mother said icily.

DUE DATE

-Jacey-

For two months, Caleb and Will put their heads together and whispered about how we could possibly get out. And for two months, they came up empty.

My water broke in the middle of the night seven weeks after our recapture. Or re-kidnapping. Or whatever it was called.

Caleb called for Will, and they both decided maybe this would be the opportunity they were looking for as I started having contractions.

But, as usual, Mr. Masterson had thought of everything. As Caleb held one of my hands and Will the other, a whole crew of doctors and nurses, with equipment, arrived in our bedroom.

"This is exciting," Mr. Masterson said, coming in himself. "And before you say you don't want me here, remember, Caleb is still expendable."

I shut my mouth. So did Caleb and Will.

"Can she have an epidural?" Caleb asked when I started crushing both their hands trying not to cry out. I didn't want to give Mr. Masterson the satisfaction.

I expected Mr. Masterson to say 'no,' but instead he shrugged. "Go ahead and give her the epidural. We want this to go as smoothly as possible."

The anesthesiologist approached me, and Caleb and Will leaned me forward. I felt a pinch in my back, but after it took effect, there was nothing but pressure. No more body-wracking pain.

"All right then," the doctor said. "I need you to be brave, Mama. You push when I tell you to, okay?"

Will and Caleb kept holding my hands. "You're going to do great," Will said.

"I'm here. Don't worry," Caleb added.

"We're going to need to get some support behind her," the doctor continued.

Caleb let go of my hand and I whimpered, but then he moved to sit behind me with my back to his chest, sitting me up just enough to be in position.

Will kept a hold of my other hand.

"Okay, let's see how much further we've progressed here," the doctor murmured, pushing up my long T-shirt and checking between my legs. "Oh good, you're crowning. I'm going to need you to push."

I looked at Will, who nodded encouragingly. Caleb kissed my hair. "Go ahead, baby. Push."

I took a deep breath and bore down, feeling an increased pressure between my legs.

"That's good. Keep pushing. Deep breaths," the doctor said. "One more time… there we go. We've got the head out."

I panted and Will took a cloth from a nurse and wiped my forehead.

"You're doing so good, baby," Caleb cooed at me, and I didn't know if I wanted to slap him or hug him.

"Okay, now we need to clear the shoulders. You give me one more good push, Jocelyn," the doctor continued.

"It's not over yet?" I all but whined.

"Just another good push or two should do it. You're doing beauti-fully," the doctor said kindly.

I groaned and took a deep breath then pushed again. Hard.

"Oh good, shoulders are out. Good job, Mama." There was a loud squall, and all of a sudden, there was a very angry Will Jr. sitting in the doctor's arms.

"He's beautiful," the three of us said together.

"Now, which one of you is Daddy? I'm sure he'd like to have the honor of cutting the cord," the doctor suggested.

Mr. Masterson stepped forward then. "I'm afraid Grandpa will be doing the honors. Thank you very much, Doctor." Mr. Masterson cut the cord with an unnecessary flourish. "Now we just need to get him cleaned up and off to the wet nurse."

"Wet nurse?" Will, Caleb, and I protested together.

"You didn't think I was going to leave him here to have your bad influence, did you?" Mr. Masterson scoffed.

I made a strangled sound in my throat. "Don't take away my son, please!"

"Father…" Will pleaded.

"Shut up." Mr. Masterson glared at each of us in turn. "Remember, I can always change my mind about Caleb."

I choked on a sob and turned my face into Caleb's shoulder.

"I hope you die in some horrible, slow, painful way," Caleb spat at Mr. Masterson.

Mr. Masterson chuckled. "I know. Now, in six weeks, we're going to start this process all over again."

"Can't we please do in vitro again, Father?" Will asked.

"You lost that privilege when you tried to escape from me," Mr. Masterson said flatly.

The nurse finished cleaning up Will Jr. and handed him to Mr. Masterson, who smiled down at my son and tickled his chin.

"You're going to be much better than your daddy," Mr. Masterson said to him.

Will Jr. squawked.

"Ah yes. Let's get you to your new nursery, shall we?" Mr. Masterson cradled Will Jr. to him and headed for the door.

"Please, Dad," Will said as I cried my eyes out.

"Don't try to butter me up. Oh, Caleb, I will be needing my

assistant back. I'm getting you an apartment close to work. I'll send Jacey there when she's pregnant again," Mr. Masterson informed us.

Will's eyes widened, and Caleb swore. "You can't keep doing this, Masterson," Caleb argued.

"Watch me." Mr. Masterson left with Will Jr.

I tried very hard not to think of the plans we'd made for raising Will Jr. I didn't want to think about the nursery in Arizona or anything like that. But the thoughts started creeping in the second Will Jr. was gone. I felt as though my heart had been torn from my body.

"I'm sorry, Jacey," Will said softly.

I couldn't stand it anymore. "Stop being sorry and *do* something!" I screamed at Will.

Will stiffened then looked at Caleb.

"Maybe you should just step out for a minute," Caleb suggested to Will. "We'll work this out."

Will nodded sadly and let go of my hand, stepping out of our room.

"Why didn't you find a way out before now?!" I then yelled at Caleb. "Why did you let this happen?!" I beat on his thighs with my fists. "How could you let him take our baby away?!"

"I'm sorry," Caleb said, hugging me tightly. If he hadn't been holding me so tightly, I would have come apart. "I'm so sorry. I know. I know we should have figured it out by now."

"Now he's sending you away. What am I supposed to do while you're gone?!" I wailed. "What am I supposed to do without you?!"

Caleb was silent for a long time. Then he sighed and dropped his chin on my shoulder. "I will make sure that Will takes care of you."

"But he's not you!" I wailed.

"No. He's not. But I want you to let him in, okay?" Caleb said, his voice hoarse. "Let him take care of you."

"You mean sex, too, don't you," I whispered.

"Yes. I mean sex, too. Don't get Masterson angry. We will figure a way out of this, but it's going to take longer than four to six weeks, I think," Caleb replied quietly. But he sounded defeated.

"You don't think we'll ever get out," I accused him.

Caleb's breath hitched. "I don't want to say that out loud, Jacey. Please don't make me."

And just like that, my last shred of hope shriveled and died.

"Caleb…" I hiccuped a sob. "He's not you."

"I know, baby. I know," Caleb said mournfully. "But he's a good man, and it's the only way we'll get to see each other again."

I tiredly squared my shoulders. One of us wasn't going to lose hope. "I won't do it," I informed both men. "And Caleb Killeen, you'll be lucky to ever get lucky again for even suggesting it."

Caleb let out a sad, strangled laugh. "There's my girl." He stroked my hair. "I just need you to be okay while I'm gone."

"You don't think Mr. Masterson is taking you away right this second, do you?" I gasped.

The doctor and nurses had quietly left, leaving just us.

"I think Masterson is capable of it," Caleb replied. "I think—"

"Caleb?" Will said, popping his head in. "I really hate to interrupt, but my father's sent his goons to take you to the apartment."

I gripped Caleb's sweatpants, refusing to let him go. "No! No, Caleb is staying. He's staying with me!" I shrieked.

Two muscled men elbowed their way past Will and into our bedroom. "The boss says we're allowed to give her a sedative if she freaks out. I think this counts as freaking out."

The other goon took out a filled syringe.

"Leave me alone! Leave us alone!" I couldn't stop screaming. I turned and clutched Caleb's T-shirt, digging my nails in. "You can't have him! You can't!"

"Jacey…" Caleb tried to sooth me. He gently tugged at my wrists, but I wouldn't let go of his shirt.

"Sedative it is." The goon with the syringe approached the bed.

"Just give me a minute!" Caleb snapped. Then he turned to me. "Baby, I don't want you to be asleep and helpless while I'm gone. Just let me go. You'll see me soon."

I sobbed, clinging to Caleb. "Please, don't go."

"I have to, baby. Or it's going to mean a lot of pain for somebody, and I don't want that somebody to be you." Caleb carefully pried my fingers out of his shirt. "Just lay down and rest, okay? You need to recover. You just gave birth."

"What, so Will can fuck me?" I sneered.

Caleb winced, a tear rolling down his cheek. "Please, Jacey. Let's not separate with us fighting."

I cried harder than I could ever remember crying in my life.

Caleb pulled me to him and kissed me, his tears mingling with mine. "It'll only be for a few weeks. Will is going to take care of you. It's going to be okay."

My sobs became broken when Caleb let me go. He stood. "Don't use that needle on her. I'm up. Let's go."

The goon with the syringe capped it again and slid it into his pocket.

I reached for Caleb as they started for the door, but then Will was there holding me back in a strong hug.

"It'll just be a few weeks," Will reassured me. "I'll stay here with you so you're not alone, okay? I'll do everything in my power to stop anything bad from happening to you or your family."

As Caleb disappeared from my sight, I just trembled, feeling completely unmoored. "What about our son?" I asked.

"I'll talk to my father about him. I don't think it'll do any good, so don't get your hopes up. But I'll try," Will said.

I liked it. Will wasn't going to tell me pretty little lies. Only Caleb was allowed to do that. "Four to six weeks, huh?"

"Yes," Will responded. "We have four to six weeks to figure it all out."

I didn't want four to six weeks. I didn't want four to six days. I just wanted to get it over with so I could go to Caleb. "What are we going to do in four to six weeks?" I asked, my voice having lost all color.

"We'll just live. We'll get to know each other better, and we'll just do the best we can," Will said. "Maybe we can get your dad to reconcile with you, I don't know."

"What makes you think I want to reconcile at this point?" I whispered.

"Because he's your dad, and you want to be able to see Timothy from time to time. Plus, it'll be hard to include them in any plans if it looks weird when we suddenly start talking to them," Will replied.

"Oh." I looked Will in the eyes. "You still think there's a possibility we can all get out of this?"

"I have to. Otherwise, I might kill myself," Will confessed.

I wrapped my arms around Will, hugging him back tightly. "Don't do that. Don't even think about it."

"It's hard not to," Will sighed. "But I'm trying to stay positive. It's just a bad situation that I can't see my way out of right now."

Maybe it was my turn to be the liar. "We'll get out of here. Somehow."

Will chuckled mirthlessly. "Thanks, Jacey. But like my father said, you're a terrible liar."

BACK IN THE OFFICE

-Caleb-

Masterson, of course, had me back in the office the very next day, even though I felt as though my heart had been ripped from my chest, and the bastard was playing hacky sack with it. I tried not to glare at him from my desk when he passed back and forth during the day.

He also got me working immediately on his more nefarious undertakings. I thought Masterson got a little giggle out of me having to deal with the illegal logging operations he had throughout the world, given it was running into the illegal logging operation he had in Canada that had first put Jacey and me on his radar.

I'd been hoping Masterson would bring Will Jr. to the office, but that silver lining wasn't coming, either. Masterson left Will Jr. wherever he'd put him. I wondered if the baby was just in another part of the mansion in Minnetonka. There was no way of knowing.

"Caleb, see that these shipments made it to their destinations, will you? There's a lad." Masterson grinned at me, handing me a folder.

I'd noticed that Masterson's less-than-legal business ventures were mostly kept on paper, rather than tracked in the computer system.

Luckily, I was able to use my computer to track the shipping containers Masterson wanted to know about.

It didn't take me long to figure out these shipments were not about trafficking illegally procured trees. These shipments were about trafficking illegally procured humans.

My stomach dropped, and I wanted to throw up. That son of a bitch.

"How's it going, Caleb?" Masterson asked, a wide grin on his face when he stuck his head out of his office.

I wanted to punch him. Desperately. I wanted to punch him and keep punching him until he was dead. "Your 'shipments' all passed inspection and made it to their destinations," I said between my teeth.

"Wonderful! I knew you'd be interested in that sort of thing." Masterson's eyes crinkled at the corners. He was overjoyed at my discomfort.

I tried to plaster my usual smile on my face, but without Jacey there for inspiration, my smile flattened into a thin line. "Anything else you want me to look into?"

"Yes. There's a shipment we lost. I want to make sure all the merchandise was destroyed," Masterson said.

"Destroyed?" I echoed, feeling bile rise in the back of my throat.

"Yes. Destroyed. You know what I mean." Masterson's gaze turned hard, and I remembered that I was expendable.

If I was killed, then there would be no one left but Will to take care of Jacey. And, quite frankly, given the fear of God his father had struck in him, I wasn't sure how good a protector Will could be. "I know what you mean," I responded obediently.

"Excellent. If the merchandise was not all destroyed, let me know right away. We wouldn't want it falling into the wrong hands." Masterson dropped a number on my desk.

With trepidation flowing through me, I called the number.

"This is Mr. William Masterson's office," I said when someone picked up but was silent. "I'm Caleb, his assistant. He wanted to make sure the merchandise from the lost shipment was all destroyed."

"Just about," a dark voice replied.

I heard a scream and then a gurgle.

"Now it's all destroyed," the man said. "You can tell Masterson he doesn't need to worry."

"Yes, sir," I responded. "Thank you, sir."

The line cut out.

I had just enough time to grab my trash can before hurling up the toast and juice I'd managed to force down that morning.

"I take it I have good news?" Masterson asked.

I wondered if he'd been standing there the whole time, giddy like a child at Christmas, waiting to see my reaction. "Yes. Good news," I rasped.

"Great. Call down to the maintenance staff to take care of that. You're not sick, are you? If you're sick, you should go home." Masterson dangled the bait.

There was no way I was giving this bastard the satisfaction of seeing me turn tail and run. "No, I'm fine. Food poisoning."

Masterson gave me an evil smile. "That's good to hear."

I knew my day of challenges was not over by a long shot.

Not an hour later, Masterson interrupted me again. "Caleb, I need you to come take dictation."

This couldn't be good. "Yes, Mr. Masterson," I said, getting out a notebook and pen. I walked into Masterson's office and stood next to his desk, waiting.

"Lacy," he said over the intercom, "I need you to come to my office. Make sure you've got coverage for an hour."

I dropped my pen to the floor. "I won't do that."

"Maybe not today. But I'll wear you down." Masterson smiled as Lacy entered his office. "Ready to make a hundred thousand dollars, Lacy?"

"Yes, sir," Lacy replied, starting to unbutton her blouse.

"I'm leaving," I said. "Turns out I am sick." I bent to pick up my pen, then stalked toward the door, handing the tablet and pen to Lacy on my way.

Masterson laughed at my back. "I knew I could find your limit."

"Yep, watching you seduce our administrative assistant is definitely my limit," I replied flatly.

"I thought it might be. Poor Caleb. You're about to become my favorite toy," Masterson chortled.

I just kept walking. A wall of muscle peeled away from the wall and followed me out. I ignored them and went to the nearest gas station to pick up crackers and clear lime soda. I wasn't sure I was going to be able to keep anything else down.

When I returned to the apartment, I was automatically locked inside. On the one hand, I hoped the locks were set to unlock if there was a fire or some other emergency. On the other hand…

I shook myself. I would not concede defeat. Not yet.

My gilded cage was complete with a large television that took up most of one wall in the living room. I sat in front of it and decided I might as well watch a movie. Maybe it would take my mind off everything I'd helped with today. Every dark deed.

I turned on the television and jumped. There, on the screen, was Jacey.

Of course, she couldn't see me, but she was resting in bed and looking despondently off into the distance. I touched the screen, willing her to glance up at the camera, but she didn't.

The door to the room opened, and Will came inside with a tray of food. Jacey just looked at it and then turned her head away.

Will sat down on the edge of the bed, and I could tell he was encouraging her to eat.

Finally, Jacey took a nibble of what looked like toast.

I relaxed and sat down, watching as Jacey ate. Masterson was an evil, evil man, letting me see Jacey like this but not be able to speak to her.

Once she'd eaten, I watched Will take the tray away. When he came back, he laid next to her on the bed.

This part I couldn't watch. Will was no doubt going to do whatever it took to make sure when he and Jacey coupled, it wouldn't be a traumatic experience for her. It's what I wanted him to do. But jealousy broiled in my gut just the same, and I tried to change the channel.

It changed, but just to another camera in the room.

Frowning, I tried changing the channel three or four more times, but it just kept switching camera angles of Will snuggling up to Jacey.

Finally, I pressed the red button to turn the whole works off. Only it didn't turn off. The television still displayed Jacey with Will.

"Oh, you bastard," I murmured, realizing Masterson had done this deliberately. He wanted me to watch the love of my life cozying up to another man.

I was his new favorite toy, after all.

I looked around the apartment and located one of the cameras I knew he had in here. I flipped the camera the bird.

Then I headed to the bedroom to lay down.

Of course, there was a TV in there as well. Without prompting, it flickered to life the second I walked in the room.

"Sonofabitch," I muttered.

I thought of going in the bathroom to escape the televisions only to remember there was one in there as well.

I was trapped with Jacey, and yet, without her.

I wanted to scream. But today, I wouldn't. Today, I still had the strength to not give Masterson what he wanted.

He wanted to break me.

I looked at Jacey lying on the bed, waiting for me to save her, and balled my hands into fists.

Masterson was never going to break me. Never.

I went into the kitchen and got a sharp knife. The living room television was mounted into the wall, but that wouldn't stop me from dealing with the others. First, I cut the cord on the kitchen television. Then the bedroom. Then the bathroom.

Satisfied, I sat down in the kitchen and had my soda and crackers. Doubtless, after work tomorrow, the TVs will be restored to working order. But right now, today, I'd won a small victory.

I wished I could say the same for the 'merchandise' on the 'lost shipment.' I now had more nightmare fuel. There had been the most awful scraping sound, I remembered now, before the gurgle.

Had it been a woman? A child?

I put down the cracker I'd been about to take a bite out of and ran to the bathroom, reaching the toilet just in time to throw up everything I'd just tried to eat. Perhaps everything I'd eaten in the last month.

I leaned my head against the toilet tank when I was finished dry heaving. Jacey. I had to think of Jacey. I had to find some way of saving us all.

After that, I was going to go to the police and try to find someone else like Darren who was willing to throw the book at Masterson. I'd get Jacey and Will Jr. to safety and then turn myself over to the law as a witness against Masterson. He had to be stopped.

I was not going to listen to another person get offed over the phone again. Not if I could help it.

WHERE THERE'S A WILL

-Jacey-

The days passed too slowly and too quickly at the same time. I missed Caleb terribly. and no matter how much Will pleaded with his father, I hadn't seen Will Jr. once.

At four weeks to the day since I gave birth, Mr. Masterson finally appeared in our bedroom. My heart sank when I saw he didn't have Will Jr. with him.

"It seems the time has come," Mr. Masterson grinned at Will and me as we poked our heads up over the covers. "Four weeks. Get to it."

"Four to six weeks, Father." Will stifled a yawn to give his father a serious look.

"I've decided four was perfectly sufficient. Now get to it," Mr. Masterson repeated.

"What, in front of you?" Will gaped.

Mr. Masterson sat down in a chair beside the bed. "Yes."

I scooted across the bed away from Will and Mr. Masterson. That left me trapped in a corner, but there was nowhere else to go.

"Jacey, I'm disappointed. You had four weeks to get your mind around the idea of what was going to happen next, and it seems you didn't use that time wisely," Mr. Masterson tsked.

"Dad, please, a little privacy," Will said, offering me a pillow to cover myself. I'd only been allowed lingerie and bikinis since Caleb was taken.

Mr. Masterson eyed us, then rose, much to my relief. "I'll let you do it one time without me watching. But I'll be back. Get her settled." He looked at Will sharply. "Don't disappoint me."

"Yeah, fine, okay," Will replied. "Just go away. Please."

With a warning expression, Mr. Masterson left.

Will sat there awkwardly while I stood in the corner, equally awkwardly We were both silent.

"He's going to the security office to watch us on camera," Will told me.

"I kind of figured," I said softly.

"We don't have a lot of time," Will continued.

"Will… I can't. I don't have anything against you. You're just not Caleb," I whispered.

"I know." Will stood up and headed for the bathroom. "I'll be out in a bit. You just sit tight."

There was something funny in his voice. "Will, are you okay?" I asked.

Will gave me a crooked smile that didn't reach his eyes. "I sure am. Better than I've been in a long time."

"Okay," I said uncertainly.

Will went into the bathroom and closed the door. I heard the big jacuzzi tub running.

I was grateful Will was giving me as much time as he could. I knew, eventually, Mr. Masterson would be back.

My hands shook as I put the pillow back down on the bed and sat on the edge of the mattress. I didn't know how I was going to let Will get on top of me and stick his dick in me. I didn't want to make the experience traumatic for either of us, but I just couldn't imagine doing anything like that with anyone but Caleb.

I sniffled and tried very hard to hold back my tears. I wished Caleb were there.

After about an hour, with no sign of Will, I was about to knock on the bathroom door and check on him when Mr. Masterson barged in himself.

"Bath time's over, William," Mr. Masterson growled. "And just for taking advantage of my good will, I am going to—" he tried the bathroom door handle and it rattled ineffectively. "What the hell? You think barricading yourself in the bathroom is going to put me in a better mood?!"

"Will," I called, frightened for him. "Just come out. We'll-We'll figure this out somehow."

Mr. Masterson rattled the knob again. "Oh, William. If you think your legs were bad…" He put his shoulder to the door and started banging into it.

The door shook on its hinges but held. It was a rather high-quality oak door.

"Damn that child!" Mr. Masterson took out his phone. "This is Masterson. I need a locksmith or a very beefy thug right now in the Killeen room. RIGHT NOW."

I huddled myself back in the corner with the pillow protecting my modesty as a handful of men quickly came in. One knelt with what I could only assume was a lock-pick set and began working on the door.

The knob finally clicked, and Mr. Masterson turned the handle and pushed, but the door still wouldn't budge.

A very beefy security man cracked his knuckles and replaced Mr. Masterson at the door. With a grunt and two slams of his shoulder, the door opened with a cracking sound.

"He barricaded the door with a chair from the make-up table, sir," the beefy thug said, holding the door open for Mr. Masterson. "Please be careful of the debris."

"I'm going to take the debris and shove it up his rebellious little ass," Mr. Masterson promised. "Do you hear me, Will? I'm-Will?"

I craned my head. Mr. Masterson's voice cracked when he said it again. "Will?"

"Get a doctor!" the big thug yelled.

"Will, you goddamn stupid son of a bitch. What have you *done?!*" Mr. Masterson screamed.

I heard water slosh onto the floor. It soaked across the tile until I could see it myself. The puddle was a deep pink.

"Will!" I shrieked, understanding now what he must have been doing while I'd been trying to prepare myself to have sex with him.

"Will!" Mr. Masterson howled, rage and something else making him hoarse.

"Stay out of the way!" the hefty thug ordered me, shoving me back to the other side of the bed.

The bloody water started to seep out across the hardwood floor of the bedroom itself.

A great deal of sloshing ensued. I supposed they were getting him out of the tub. I felt so helpless, dumbly sitting there, clutching a pillow.

In a matter of minutes, the same doctor who had delivered Will Jr. came pelting into the bedroom, then raced into the bathroom, slipping on the pink water.

I crawled to the edge of the bed again, trying to see what was going on. I couldn't see, but I could hear.

"He's not breathing," Mr. Masterson said.

There was a pause, and then the doctor replied, "Continue CPR. Olaf, get a nurse to bring some type B negative blood. We'll need to replenish what he's lost."

"He's still not breathing!" Mr. Masterson yelled.

"Sir, I'm going to need you to calm down," the doctor said. "I'm going to do everything I can, but your son has lost a lot of blood. For now, keep pressure on his wrists."

My hands flew to my mouth. Will had slit his wrists?!

A few minutes later, a nurse ran in holding IV bags of blood. "I can't find a vein," she told the doctor, frustrated.

"He's not breathing," Mr. Masterson repeated.

"No," the doctor said. "He's not. Nurse, don't bother. Time of death 10:43 AM. Call for an ambulance pickup."

"Dead? My son is dead?" Mr. Masterson hissed.

"There's nothing else to be done, Mr. Masterson," the doctor replied sadly.

There was a clatter and two more security guards rushed into the bathroom. "Mr. Masterson! Mr. Masterson, you need to calm down, sir!"

"I am going to snap your damn neck!" Mr. Masterson shouted, and I heard a gurgle.

Oh God. Oh God, Will was dead. And the doctor was next.

"Mr. Masterson, get a hold of yourself!" the big thug said. "Think of the cops!"

"Bury him in the woods, six feet deep. I don't want anyone or anything ever finding him again," Mr. Masterson responded angrily.

"Your son, sir?" the thug asked.

"No. The doctor." Then there was a loud bang. A gun blast.

I went back to my corner, scrunching up as small as possible. The doctor was dead. Would Mr. Masterson kill me, too?

"Sir, people will miss him. It would be better if—" the thug began.

"I don't care. Do as I say. I want him buried in an unmarked grave for all eternity," Mr. Masterson said.

The thug sighed. "Yes, sir." He stepped outside the bathroom.

The lifeless body of the doctor was slung over his shoulder. I stared in horror.

"As for William, I will need to make arrangements," Mr. Masterson sniffed. "We'll use the same funeral home that we used for his mother. They did an excellent job."

"The doctor said we need to get an ambulance first," one of the security guards said. "I worry what will happen if we don't follow protocol."

"Then call the coroner we know. I don't want it known far and wide that Masterson's son killed himself." Mr. Masterson came out of the bathroom then. He was covered in pink, bloody water.

I made myself smaller still, hoping to escape his notice. But he looked right at me.

"Get rid of her," he growled.

"Sir?" the remaining security guards asked.

"You know what I mean. Just get rid of her." Mr. Masterson waved a hand vaguely in my direction.

The thugs closed in on me. I backed flat to the wall, but there was nowhere to go.

One of them picked me up, and I screamed and kicked and lashed out with my fingernails.

"Do you want to be buried in an unmarked grave, too?" the security guard grunted.

Trembling, I replied, "No."

"Then knock it off," he said.

I looked around at the others and saw one was already getting out a syringe.

I stopped resisting. "I'll be good. Please just make sure Caleb has a place he can visit me." Tears ran down my cheeks.

The guard carrying me grunted again, and then the three of them carried me out to a black sedan that had already pulled out in front of the mansion.

When the guards opened the trunk, I started struggling again. Inside was a shovel, rope, duct tape, a saw... anything and everything I could imagine that would be used to dismember and dispose of a body.

"Throw her in already," the thug commanded the other guards.

The next thing I knew, I was in the trunk with a shovel biting into my back.

That wasn't the worst thing, though. The worst thing was that they duct taped my mouth, wrists, and ankles.

And then threw the doctor's body in next to me.

I screamed through the duct tape, but of course, no one could hear me. The trunk closed, and I was left in the dark.

As we drove over the packed gravel drive, the doctor's body bumped against me. I sobbed, wondering what my fate would be.

The car drove for a long time. After a while, the sedan hit bumpy ground then stopped. The trunk opened, and the four guards were there.

"Don't do anything stupid like start kicking out the taillights. I can still drop you in the river," the thug informed me. He grabbed the shovel and handed it to one of the guards. Then he heaved up the doctor.

The trunk slammed shut again.

I wondered if I should try to draw attention to my predicament anyway, but the sound of shovel hitting dirt told me I probably shouldn't.

We were there for what must have been hours. I tried hard not to cry. I tried very hard. I just wasn't successful.

The trunk lid opened again, and the thug threw in the shovel, sprinkling me with dirt. "Now, you."

I screamed behind my duct tape gag, but the thug just grinned and shut the trunk lid. I sat in the dark, praying for Caleb. If I was expendable now, then he surely was as well.

The next time I saw daylight, it was actually overhead fluorescents.

"Hup," the thug said and hefted me over his shoulder, duct tape and all.

We were in a parking garage. I had no idea where.

Wherever it was, the residents knew better than to bat an eyelash when they saw four guards carrying a bound woman getting on the elevator. One lady even suddenly got very interested in her dog.

"Help," I begged behind my gag. But it just came out as, "Hmph!"

We went up several floors then stopped on the thirty-second. The guards used a keypad next to room 3202, and the door sprung open.

I was unceremoniously dumped on the floor.

"Good luck," the thug chuckled then closed the door behind him.

I waited three beats, listening for their retreating footsteps down the hall, then wriggled over to the door and used it to help me sit up. I jiggled the handle, but it was no use. Whatever this room was, it was locked from the outside.

I leaned back against the door, wondering how long I could barricade myself in using just my body.

There was a clock on a table near the door, and I watched as half an hour ticked by. Five-thirty PM.

A series of footsteps approached the door.

I closed my eyes and braced my feet against the wall.

When the keypad beeped the code and the door released, I tensed all my muscles, determined to fight until the very end.

The door opened just a crack, but it was enough.

"Jacey?" Caleb breathed. "What are you doing here?"

LOCKED IN

-Caleb-

The first thing I noticed was that the door wasn't opening. At least not much. This made the guard next to me scowl.

What I saw next made my heart beat fast. Jacey. My Jacey was in my apartment.

Sitting on the floor. Duct taped, in her lingerie nightie, with her mouth covered.

Rage simmered in my gut. "What the hell, guys? Who left her duct taped on my floor, huh?"

The guards just chuckled.

"Jacey, love, let me in," I murmured, trying to reduce the fear in her eyes.

She finally recognized me, and her eyes welled up with tears.

"Jacey, honey, you need to get away from the door," I said kindly.

Jacey nodded and rolled away across the wood floor so I could swing the door open. One guard came in behind me carrying a vetted bag of groceries.

I knelt next to Jacey, ignoring him. "Baby, let me get the duct tape off you, okay?"

Jacey nodded again.

I took her hands in mine and started at her wrists.

The guard tossed down a bottle of Goo Gone and then left the apartment, still chuckling. The door closed behind him with a low beep, telling me we'd both been locked in.

Since I didn't want to hurt her, I began using the Goo Gone as I peeled back the duct tape.

"Mmm," Jacey said, shaking her head and working her jaw.

"Oh. Sorry." I very gently removed the duct tape from her mouth.

Jacey took a deep gulp of air then threw herself at me, sobbing into my dress shirt.

"Baby. Baby, I'm here. It's okay," I murmured, gathering her in my arms.

Jacey shook her head. "It's not okay," she croaked.

"What's the matter, baby? Are you… pregnant?" I asked delicately.

"No. Will slit his wrists." Jacey heaved a sob. "He's dead."

"Dead?!" On the one hand, that meant he couldn't screw my Jacey, but on the other, he was my best friend. And he was dead.

"Yes," Jacey replied hoarsely, hammering a spike of sadness and regret into my chest with that one word.

I stroked Jacey's hair and back, trying to comfort her while I sorted out my own feelings. "He was a good man," I said softly.

"It's my fault," Jacey whispered through her tears.

"How do you figure that?" I asked, frowning.

"I should have just let him. I should have been willing," Jacey cried.

I took Jacey by the shoulders and pulled her away just enough so I could look in her beautiful green eyes. "Jacey, that's not true. If anything, this is Masterson's fault. He was trying to force both of you to do something you didn't want to do."

Jacey's eyes filled with fresh tears. "Mr. Masterson was so angry. He killed the doctor. I thought he was going to kill me, too. I still think he might. Both of us."

I pulled Jacey against me again. "I don't know, baby. But I do know I love you, and now that you're here, we can face whatever comes together."

Jacey clung to me, and I kissed her hair. I buried my nose in it, drawing a deep breath. This was my Jacey. She was here, in my arms.

Then I remembered the duct tape. "Here, love. Let's get the rest of this duct tape off of you."

With a wet sniffle, Jacey held out her wrists again. I worked the duct tape off with the Goo Gone.

I did the same with her ankles.

Jacey straddled me, and I held her close, the fabric of her lingerie slippery under my fingers. I trailed my fingertips over the vast expanses of bare skin between scraps of lace.

"Caleb?" Jacey asked softly while I splayed my fingers low on her back and thought about how she was mine. I didn't have to share her with Will. And then the selfish thought tunneled a hole in my stomach. My thoughts went back and forth that way.

"Caleb?" Jacey said again.

I pulled myself out of my thoughts. "Yes, my love?"

"Do you... want to?" Jacey asked, her lower lip trembling, her eyes vulnerable.

She needed the grounding and escape that came with sex. So did I.

"I don't have any condoms," I told her.

It hung in the air between us.

Jacey stroked my cheek. "That's okay," she finally decided. "It... it would be okay if..."

"Oh, baby, I love you," I murmured and kissed her.

Jacey started unbuttoning my shirt. I helped with the cuffs blindly, both of us fumbling as we tried to kiss and strip at the same time.

"I love you, too," Jacey said when we came up for air.

We didn't stay that way for long. I bunched up my shirt and put it behind her head as I laid her back on the wood floor. "Baby, is this okay? I don't want you to be uncomfortable, but I'm also not sure I can make it to the sofa."

Jacey undid my pants and slipped her hand inside my silk boxers. My dick strained in her hand, excited Mama was home.

I couldn't stop kissing her. I possessed her mouth with my tongue. I wanted to possess her everywhere. She was my Jacey. Mine.

I roughly pushed her panties aside and slid two fingers up inside her, making her moan into my mouth. Her need coated my fingers, but I knew this would be her first time since having a baby, and it had been only four weeks since she gave birth. So I made very sure she was ready before pushing the head of my cock up against her entrance.

"Caleb," Jacey mewled, arching for me.

I slid my hand up under her camisole and found her breast. I teased her nipple and pushed my tongue into her mouth slowly, yet desperately, the same way I pushed my cock into her body.

"Oh, baby, you feel so good," I remarked against her lips.

"Can you go slow?" Jacey asked, clinging to my bare shoulders.

"I can try. But I've missed you so much. I don't know how successful I'll be," I confessed.

"Okay." Jacey let me set the pace.

I thrust slowly and gently into her, holding back the lust that burned within me. Jacey had almost been with another man. I'd basically begged her to.

But Will had thwarted Masterson's plans with a couple of simple slices, and now Jacey was with me again.

My thrusts became deep and possessive. Jacey whimpered but hung on, wrapping her legs around my waist.

"Caleb," Jacey moaned when I moved my hand down to rub her clit.

"Baby, I'm gonna fill you up. You just come for me, okay?" I said, thrusting hard and grazing my teeth up her neck.

Jacey came with a cry, her whole body shuddering, her inner muscles gripping around my cock.

I pushed as deep as I could and spurted hot cum into her, knowing full well we might be making a baby. It gave me a whole new sense of purpose.

When I was finished, I kissed Jacey and gently pulled out. She made a sound of protest until I got to my feet and tugged her up into my arms. "Let's go somewhere a little more comfortable, shall we?" I asked.

"Okay." Jacey slid her hand into mine, and I walked her to the bedroom.

I threw back the covers, and Jacey sat down on the cool sheets. She crooked her finger at me, beckoning me.

Nothing mattered now except making love to Jacey. There was no outside world. No Masterson. No dead Will. No imprisoned parents. Only us.

And I intended to keep us on that cloud for as long as possible.

I prowled over her and kissed her. Jacey reached between us and began jerking me off, getting me hard for another go-round.

She didn't want to return to reality any more than I did.

When I was ready, I stopped her with a hand on her wrist then clasped her hands over her head while I sank into her sweet, wet warmth.

"Baby, tell me if I make you sore," I whispered against her lips as I started to thrust.

Jacey's whole body shook as this time. I didn't hold back. I needed this. We needed this.

"Kiss me," Jacey begged as I watched her breasts bounce, her nipples peaked and calling my name.

They would have to wait. I fused my lips to hers, and she sucked my tongue into her mouth while her body took my hard thrusts.

I felt her come around my cock and groaned as I found my own release, giving her my semen as deep inside her as I could go.

"I think I should get you pregnant," I panted, kissing her neck and finally able to fondle her pert nipples. "On purpose. Then maybe Masterson will stop obsessing over you."

Jacey's arms descended from over her head to wrap around my neck. "You want to give me a baby, Daddy?"

I shivered when she called me 'daddy.' It was so fucking hot. "Yeah," I said, putting my hand over her belly. "Daddy's gonna put a baby right here."

Jacey bit her lip, and her eyes swam with tears. "He or she won't be a replacement for Will Jr."

And in that moment, I remembered the biggest reason I wanted to kill Masterson—the look on Jacey's face when he took our baby away.

"I know, baby," I murmured, kissing Jacey softly. "Nothing can replace Will Jr."

"We're going to get him back someday," she said desperately. "Right?"

"We're not going to rest until we do," I reassured her.

"Good." Jacey looked at me with warm, adoring eyes. "I missed you, Caleb. So much. I hurt every day."

I kissed her. "Me, too. I hurt every day without you."

"Let's not ever be apart again," Jacey said.

I sighed. "I suppose that depends on what Masterson has in store for us."

Jacey hugged me tighter, using both arms and legs. "Let's not think about him. Not until we have to."

I grimaced. "I have to work for him tomorrow."

"Ew," Jacey responded sympathetically.

"But it will be a lot easier knowing I'll have you to come home to," I added.

"I'll be waiting," she smiled.

"I'll also probably find out more about our current situation at work tomorrow. Unless Masterson doesn't come in," I muttered.

Jacey frowned. "You'd think he'd take some time off for the death of his son."

"This is Masterson we're talking about here," I said.

"Still. I mean, even to look good in the public eye," Jacey suggested.

"I suppose there is that. I—"

There was a buzzing in my pants. I groaned, realizing I never really got them all the way off.

"I have to take this," I said to Jacey. "It's always Masterson or one of the assistants."

Jacey nodded, and I pulled the phone out and put it to my ear. "Yes?"

"Caleb. I can see you're enjoying your present." Masterson confirmed he was watching. But then, he was always watching.

"What do you want, Masterson?" I asked.

"Straight to the point. That's good." Masterson's words lacked some of their usual glee. I wondered if he really was affected some by his son's suicide. "I'm giving you the month off. I'm going to be working from home, and I know you're going to be working hard on getting our pretty little Jacey pregnant again. We have to keep up appearances, you know."

"Of course," I replied sarcastically.

"To that end, you will, of course, not be telling tales at work. Or to anyone, for that matter. I can still hurt your family," Masterson threatened.

"I kind of figured there would be a gag order in place. So, what's the plan for us? Are you going to kill us?" I asked.

Jacey squeaked underneath me.

"I haven't quite decided yet. You are a very good assistant," Masterson said.

"Great," I replied.

"And I'm sure we can find something for Jacey to do," Masterson continued.

"Well, she won't be doing you, so you can get that idea out of your head right now," I said.

I could almost hear his indifferent shrug. "It wouldn't matter if she did. I've had the snip. And I don't plan on getting it reversed just to antagonize you. I have bigger fish to fry."

"Gee, thanks," I grumbled.

"You're welcome. Speaking of bigger fish, I will need your help planning the funeral. I think you were more in touch with what Will liked," Masterson said.

I was about to return with something sarcastic, but Jacey put a hand on my arm. I blew out a long breath. "I'll do what I can."

"Wonderful. I'll forward you the details, and you can take care of the small touches," Masterson told me.

It occurred to me that Masterson knew nothing about his son. I would be the one deciding on colors and themes.

I looked down at Jacey who was stroking my arm.

"Yes, sir," I said. This was the least I could do for my friend.

THE FUNERAL

-Jacey-

I put my hand over Caleb's as we sat in the fourth row of the church, toward the middle. Caleb had done a wonderful job with the flowers, blues and whites, and Will's baseball memorabilia was sitting on and around the coffin. All in all, everything was beautiful.

The priest had been paid a large sum of money to ignore the fact that Will wasn't Catholic. According to Masterson, they weren't anything, really. But it was the only space large enough in a thirty-mile radius of their home with enough space to accommodate the big to-do Masterson wanted.

Well-wishers came to a grieving Masterson in a line that extended out of the church doors and into the street. The who's who of business were all there to pay their respects, to Masterson and not Will. But Will's old baseball team was here along with his coach. And that was something.

Masterson didn't want any scenes, so our parents weren't there. But Will Jr. was cradled in some stranger's arms who stood next to Masterson and looked appropriately stricken. I eyed my baby hungrily, but didn't dare go forward and try to take him. That would get one of my parents or Timothy killed. I'd been warned.

"Caleb?" I asked, squeezing his hand. He'd had to plan all this, right down to writing Masterson's eulogy. He'd been wrecked over it all week.

"No one here knew him. No one here actually cares," Caleb whispered, his eyes shining with unshed tears.

"We knew him," I tried to comfort him. "And his baseball team came."

"Masterson didn't even know they placed second in the nationals. Of course, he was a bit disappointed it was only second," Caleb muttered.

I shrugged. "Masterson is a…" I lowered my voice so no one around us could hear and whispered in Caleb's ear. "… dick."

"That's putting it mildly," a voice behind us slurred.

Caleb and I whirled around and saw one of the baseball team members holding a flask and looking bleary-eyed.

"Oh, she didn't mean it. Really," Caleb said quickly as we both started to sweat.

"Sure you didn't," the drunk teammate snorted. "We all knew it. Glad to know some things never change."

"Jake, I think you've had enough," the coach said, plucking the flask from his fingers. "We're here to honor our friend."

"How did you know him?" Jake asked, frowning at his hand as though wondering if the flask had vanished into thin air.

"College, actually," Caleb replied. "We were both going for a medical degree."

Jake snorted again.

"Jake…" the coach murmured in a warning tone.

"What? Will could have gone to the big leagues. He wanted to. But Daddy interfered again," Jake said nastily.

"Mr. Masterson is grieving." The coach took him by the shoulders. "Come on, let's get some air."

"I don't want air! I want Will to be happily playing for the Yankees!" Jake shouted.

Several people turned around and looked at the four of us.

"Jake," the coach hissed. "You're making a scene."

"Well, *someone* should!" he insisted, standing on his wobbly legs. "Hey! Masterson! You're a dick!"

There was a collective gasp.

Two of Jake's teammates quickly stood and helped wrangle Jake out of the pew and into the aisle. "Sorry, sir. He's drunk. He didn't mean it."

"The hell I didn't!" Jake shouted. "I want the whole fucking world to know what a controlling, absent, fucking sadistic SON OF A BITCH that man there is!" He stabbed an accusing finger in Masterson's direction.

Caleb paled and put a protective arm around me. We didn't know if this would blow back on us.

Masterson, instead, dropped his head into his hands and let out a very convincing sob. "If only I'd known he was so unhappy," he stage whispered, loud enough for the whole church to hear.

"The FUCK you didn't!" Jake yelled, even as they were dragging him out. "Let go of me, that MOTHERFUCKER needs to know!"

"Jake, stop. Stop! We're at his son's funeral, for Christ's sake!" the coach admonished him.

"What better place to tell the GODDAMN BASTARD he's the reason his son is dead!" Jake howled.

No doubt, Jake would have said more, but between his teammates and the coach, he was dragged out of the church.

There was a terrible hush then a flurry of murmurs.

Masterson spared us a glare, and Caleb shrugged helplessly.

My stomach roiled. Was he going to blame us for this?

"Ladies and gentlemen, please. The man was only speaking his truth," Masterson said, dabbing at his eyes. "And he's right. I should have been more attentive. I'm sorry. I need a moment. Caleb?"

Caleb stood, and I stood with him. He shook his head at me, but I gripped his arm, and he knew he couldn't leave without me without causing another scene.

Jaw set, Caleb escorted me to follow behind Masterson. We ended up in the bridal suite.

Caleb quietly closed the door.

"I didn't know. Honestly. He just happened to be sitting behind us," Caleb said before Masterson could start in on us.

"Oh I know that," Masterson replied. "You wouldn't dare. I want to know who the *fuck* that was, and I want you to find out now."

"I… sir, he's in a lot of pain. I'm sure they were close friends," Caleb pleaded. "Please don't do anything rash."

"I want to know what he knows, who he's telling it to, and if he has any concrete evidence," Masterson fired off. "And I want you to start right now."

Caleb swallowed. "Yes, sir."

"You two can have this room. Do whatever you need to do, but I want to have this information by the time of the interment," Masterson ordered.

"Yes, sir," Caleb repeated.

Masterson left, slamming the door shut behind him.

Caleb sank down on the loveseat and patted the spot beside him while he took out his phone. I sat down.

He guided my head into his lap and started stroking my hair while he researched with his thumb. "Jacob Ramacher."

"He was on Will's baseball team?" I asked.

"Yes. Suffered a knee injury, so he had to leave the team, but he did go to State with them," he said.

"Why is he so broken up over Will? More than the others?" I turned my head so I could see him from the corner of my eye.

He gave a long sigh. "Jacey, honey, Will was bisexual. I can only assume, with a reaction like that, that they were lovers."

"Oh no. Mr. Masterson is not going to be excited about that," I whispered.

"I was hoping he'd never find out. So was Will. But I have no real evidence that was the case, so, I don't have to float the idea past Masterson. I just have to figure out more information about Jake," he said.

"What do you think Mr. Masterson will do to him?" I asked softly.

He ran his fingers through my hair, completely messing it up. I didn't care. "I imagine he's going to punish Jake for ruining the funeral."

My face fell and I pressed my cheek into his thigh. "I don't want to be a party to that."

"I'm hoping to find out that Jake is untouchable or something redeeming about him or… something. Anything to keep Masterson from hurting him," he said.

"Work hard," I told him. "God, if it weren't for Timothy and our parents…"

"We'd have found another way by now. I know. I hate it, too," he grunted.

I placed a soft kiss on Caleb's knee. "I know you'll find something."

"Ah, here we go. Jacob Ramacher, heir to Ramacher Industries. He's untouchable. Good." He sounded relieved.

"I hope that's enough to make him untouchable," I said.

"It had better be. I can't think of anything that will protect him more than being heir to the throne, so to speak," he responded.

"Is Ramacher bigger than Masterson? The companies, I mean," I asked.

He looked over his information and his face fell. "No."

"Oh." I sat up and glanced down at Caleb's phone. "I suppose, in this case, size matters."

"Masterson could buy Ramacher if he wanted to, actually. Or do a hostile takeover. I can't imagine what that will mean for Jake," he murmured.

"Maybe Mr. Masterson will just let this one go?" I suggested dubiously.

Caleb laughed bitterly. "I don't see that happening."

I could hear music starting to play through the door and winced. I felt sort of bad missing Will's funeral, but there wasn't anything there that Caleb hadn't orchestrated, and Mr. Masterson was going to be giving a eulogy that I'd already read after Caleb wrote it, so maybe it was better that we were missing out. It wouldn't seem like such a farce.

"We could go back in, and I could tell Masterson what I know," Caleb said. "I know we're missing the funeral."

"It's a mockery of a funeral," I replied, my voice hitching on the last word.

His hand stilled in my hair. "I know, baby. I know it is."

I shook my head. "He deserved better than this."

"He did. And after we figure this out, we'll have a small gathering with just his baseball team and honor him properly," he promised.

"Okay." I snuggled into him, the hem of my skirt riding up my thigh.

His breath caught, then his warm hand was on the bare skin of my thigh. "You know," he said, trailing his thumb under the hem of my skirt. "There aren't any cameras in here."

I perked up, understanding exactly what Caleb wanted. "Should I lock the door?"

"Yes," he whispered.

I sat up and went to the door, locking it. Caleb came up behind me and wrapped me in his arms, threading his fingers through mine and pressing our joined hands against the door.

"We're going to do it here?" I asked.

Caleb's other hand pushed up my skirt and gripped my panties, snapping them at the elastic and letting them fall to the floor. "Yes, we're doing it right here."

I shivered with anticipation as I felt his knuckles brush against my ass while he pulled his zipper down.

"Legs a little wider, baby," he said and helped me kick my leg out into a wider stance.

He pressed the thick head of his dick against my entrance, and I gasped.

"Do you need some warming up?" he asked, rocking his hips so his cock rubbed right where I wanted it.

I shook my head vigorously. "I just need you."

Still, he took care when he pushed into me slowly. I made a little sound of need in my throat, and he obliged me by pushing all the way in.

I gripped his hand while he rocked gently, sliding in and out at an unhurried pace. He groaned when I began grinding back against him, seeking more friction.

"Is this how my baby wants it?" he asked, putting an arm around my middle and thrusting sharply and deeply.

"Yes," I begged. "I want more, Caleb. More."

He thrust harder and faster, and I panted and continued to ask for more. My orgasm hit me like a truck, and I dug my nails into the wood of the door while Caleb let out a moan and poured into me.

I dropped my head back onto his shoulder. "So good…"

"Yes," he agreed. "Very good." He pulled out gently, then took out a handkerchief and carefully wiped between my legs.

I curled my fingers into his lapel. "It's nice, not being watched."

"Very," he agreed. He pulled me against him and kissed me.

There was a bang at the door. "Open up, you two." I recognized one of the guards' voices.

Caleb pulled my skirt back down to my knees and zipped himself back up. Then he calmly opened the door. "I did my research," he said. "Is it time for the interment?"

"Yeah," the guard replied. "Good guess. Masterson wants the information right now. So you'd better deliver."

"I thought he might like to see Will put in the ground first," I argued.

The guard looked at me, focusing a bit too long on my chest. "Masterson wants it now. When he says he wants it now, he wants it now."

I nodded and Caleb took me by the hand and walked me out of the bridal suite. We joined mourners getting into their cars.

Masterson was there and gestured for us to join him in his limo at the head of the line.Caleb and I quickly complied.

"So," Masterson said before we were even seated. "What did you find out?"

GUNNING FOR JAKE

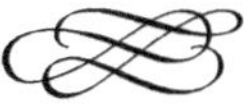

-Caleb-

I brought up the information I had on Jacob Ramacher and handed my phone to Masterson. "He's the son of Gregory Ramacher, head of Ramacher Industries."

Masterson grimaced. "What are they worth?"

"Enough to be expensive to buy, but not impossible," I said reluctantly.

"Good. Call the lawyers and tell them to make it happen," Masterson responded. He looked Jacey up and down in a way I did not like. Not that I would have liked any way he looked at Jacey. "You certainly are a miracle worker, young lady. It used to be like pulling teeth to get this one to do anything."

Jacey swallowed uncertainly. "Thank you, sir?"

"You're welcome. Sorry you missed the funeral, but it's not as though there was anything said that you hadn't already written down," Masterson said.

"True." I put an arm around Jacey. "Would you like me to make that call now, sir?"

"Yes. Oh, are they profitable?" he asked. "What about their debts?"

"They have very little debt and are very profitable," I replied.

"Excellent. Make it happen. I'll leave you two here while I go make sure they put Will in the ground properly. Make the necessary calls."

I looked around to see we were already at the cemetery. One of the guards opened the door for Masterson, who plastered on a solemn face. The guard grinned at us and closed the door, leaving Jacey and me alone.

"You're going to have to do it, aren't you?" she asked, putting a hand on my arm.

I picked up my phone from where Masterson had left it on the seat and gripped it in my lap. "Yes."

"Jake will be in a very precarious position when it's over," she said worriedly.

"You think I don't know that?!" I snapped.

Jacey recoiled, and I closed my eyes, taking several deep breaths. "Baby, I'm sorry. It's not you. It's me and this whole situation. I feel like I'm marching a guy to the guillotine."

She returned to my side then and laid her head on my shoulder. "I love you, Caleb. Nothing you do to keep us safe, to keep our family safe, is ever going to make me think less of you, okay?"

I kissed the top of her head and pressed the contact for the lawyers. Masterson was a man whose calls were taken even on the weekend.

"Hello?" a gruff voice asked when the line connected.

"Hey, Brad. It's Caleb. Masterson wants to buy Ramacher Industries. He wants it to happen as soon as possible. And it doesn't matter if they're selling or not," I said.

"Got it." Brad scribbled something down in the background. "How is Mr. Masterson? It's a terrible thing, what happened to his son."

I ground my teeth. I wished Masterson had at least the same casual sympathy toward his own son that Brad did. "He's hanging in there."

"Good. I'll talk to you when I've made the necessary arrangements." He hung up.

I set my phone down on the seat next to me and pulled Jacey into my lap, burying my face in her chest and letting out a muffled scream of frustration.

She stroked my hair and the back of my neck. "It's okay, Caleb. It's going to be okay."

When? my mind despaired, but I didn't dare share my defeatism with her. She needed hope. And I needed to keep fostering that hope.

Masterson got back in the car, and I let Jacey slide to my side once more. He grinned at us. "Can't keep your hands off each other even for a minute, huh?"

"I called Brad," I interrupted whatever sick path he was going down. "He said he'll make it happen and get back to me when all is ready."

"Good." Masterson licked his lips and looked at Jacey's exposed calves. "You truly are a beautiful woman, Jacey."

Her face flushed. "I… um… thank you, sir?"

I removed my suit jacket and casually draped it over her legs. "Wouldn't want you to get distracted, sir."

She gave my hand a grateful squeeze.

"Of course." He yawned. "Ugh, it's been a long day. Funerals are so tedious, don't you think?"

"I suppose," I replied through gritted teeth.

"I'm glad I didn't have to plan any of it." He leaned back and closed his eyes. "We'll be dropping you at the apartment first."

"Where is Will Jr.?" Jacey blurted.

I winced, but I also wanted to know, so I was also proud of her for asking.

Masterson peeked an eye open. "With his nurse, of course."

"Am I ever going to get to see him?" she asked.

"No," Masterson responded. "Now let me sleep."

Jacey drew a sharp breath and turned her face into my shoulder. I knew she was trying not to cry.

Masterson was soon snoring.

I thought of suffocating him with my shirt. Or breaking one of the scotch tumblers in the back of the limo and slitting his throat. But the guards were keeping a close watch from the front of the limo, as the partition was down. There would be no opportunity to finish the job.

Instead, I stroked Jacey's hair and plotted a million and one useless ideas about how to kill Masterson. The biggest problem was that his guards were always there. Watching. Waiting. Doing his bidding.

We pulled into the apartment complex, and two of the guards got out of the limo to escort Jacey and me to our apartment. The last one stayed with Masterson.

"You kids have fun," one of the guards snickered before locking us in.

Jacey was still quiet. I hugged her and rubbed her arms, trying to get a little life back in her. "Hey, baby. I'm sorry about Will Jr."

Jacey looked up at me with wide, wounded eyes. "I don't want Will going to the other side knowing his child is in the hands of a monster."

"I don't, either. But an opportunity we can use just hasn't presented itself," I sighed.

"I know." She shook her head. "I feel so trapped, Caleb."

"We'll find a way," I reassured her, even though I wasn't sure I believed it myself anymore. "Together, there is nothing we can't do."

She sniffled. "Thanks."

"You're welcome, baby." I rubbed her back and kissed her forehead.

"But I know you don't believe it," she continued.

I stiffened. "I mean, sure I do…"

"Please don't lie to me, Caleb," she whispered.

My shoulders fell in defeat. "I don't see a way out."

"Will found a way out," she replied quietly.

I felt my heart seize in my chest, and I pushed her away from me, holding her at arm's length. "Don't," I said. "Don't you dare. Don't you even *think* it!"

Tears streamed down Jacey's cheeks. "Then what else are we going to do?"

Determination swelled in me. I might not believe it could be done, but I had to try to get us out if Jacey was so far gone she was thinking of doing something that stupid. "I tell you what," I responded. "If I can't get us out within a year, we'll revisit this, okay? But either way, we go together."

"Okay." She stepped into my arms again and tucked her head under my chin.

I couldn't imagine this bright, brilliant woman dying at the tender age of nineteen. I was just going to have to step it up a notch.

"I love you, Jacey," I said quietly.

"I love you, too, Caleb," she replied with a sniffle.

That decided, I brought Jacey to the sofa. "If Masterson has given us cable or something instead of just the all-Caleb-and-Jacey-sex channel, I think we should watch a movie and just unwind, okay?"

"I can try," she said. She sat down on the sofa, and I sat next to her, snuggling her into my side and pulling a blanket up around us.

Mercifully, Masterson had gotten tired of tormenting me with images of Jacey and Will in bed together, so we did have a few channels to choose from.

I put on a rom-com and leaned my cheek against Jacey's hair while her head was resting on my shoulder.

"Remember the last time we did this?" she asked wistfully.

"The last thing we watched, I think, was an action movie, and we weren't really watching it at all," I recalled.

"No. When we just sat under a blanket together?" she clarified.

I smiled at her and kissed her nose. "It was before your dad knew about us."

Under the blanket, Jacey pulled down my zipper. "We did something very private."

I groaned as she circled my cock with her fist, releasing me from my boxers. "We did," I agreed. "Then we went to our bedrooms–I can't even remember whose we chose–and finished what we started."

"Nobody's here to stop us now," she said, pumping her hand up and down my shaft just the way I liked it. "And I'm still not wearing underwear."

That fact made something in my head snap. I pulled her into my lap and sank into her warmth.

She gasped and gripped my shoulders. She moved herself slowly up and down on my cock, and I let her decide the pace, putting my hands on her hips just to keep her balanced.

A whimper escaped her as she got close, moving faster.

I sucked her neck, groaning as we came together, my dick erupting inside her.

She cried out and then sagged against me, her arms around my neck. Both of us tried to catch our breath.

I wasn't sure what happened in the plot of the movie, but I sure as hell knew I'd enjoyed myself immensely. "Baby, that was spectacular," I murmured, kissing her shoulder.

"Me, too," she answered, and I had to laugh. She wasn't even stringing sentences together coherently.

"Do you want some water or something to eat?" I asked.

She raised her head a little. "You have the strength to go get it?"

She made a good point. I took stock of my legs and torso, then nodded. "I probably won't after what we do tonight, but right now I can get us fed."

"Okay." We both carefully got her off my dick. I helped her lie down on the sofa with the blanket over her, then kicked off my pants and boxers, going to the kitchen in just my shirt and socks.

I scared us up a plate of crackers and cheese and two water bottles then returned to the sofa.

Jacey already looked sleepy.

"Here, baby, eat something. It's been a long day," I encouraged her.

With the cutest little scrunched face, she sat up. She took the water bottle I brought her from me and then began to eat.

I ate, too. Not because I was necessarily hungry, but because I needed the sustenance.

I never knew what I was going to face at work the next day.

ESCORT SERVICE

-Jacey-

"Spend lots of time pissing him off," I told Caleb as I hugged him before he went to work.

The guard waiting in our doorway rolled his eyes. "Come on, let's be on time." He tapped his watch.

"I could start by coming in late," Caleb teased.

The guard did not take kindly to that and dragged Caleb out of my arms and out of the apartment. "He'll be back later," he said.

I scowled at him, but it didn't stop him from marching Caleb away.

When the door closed, I was left alone in the apartment. Again.

I walked around, noticing several cameras discreetly placed around the apartment. I wanted to smash them all.

At lunchtime, I went to the fridge and rummaged around a bit, but we didn't have a lot. With little choice, I opened the front door and stuck my head out. "Hey, do you guys do food delivery, or is there a chance I can go out and get some fresh air and do a little shopping?"

The guard grunted. "Mommy Dearest wants to go shopping," he said, pressing his earpiece.

'Mommy Dearest? *That* was the codename they came up with for me?!' I frowned at him.

After a few nods, the guard turned to me. "Grocery shopping only. And if you try to run or tell anyone about your situation, you are toast."

I swallowed and nodded my agreement.

The guard escorted me down the hall and to the parking garage where another guard joined him. My escort got in the back of the vehicle with me while the other guard got behind the wheel.

"What happens when we need other things? Clothes? Lightbulbs?" I asked.

"You make another request," the guard said.

I sighed and watched Minneapolis go by outside the window.

We stopped at a Lunds & Byerlys.

The guard escorting me scooted me out of the car with his hip while the driver held the door open. "Now, we're going to go in there, you're going to get the shit you need, and we're leaving," my escort said. "Got it?"

"Loud and clear," I replied. The guard handed me a basket ,and we walked around the store, me trying to fill up the basket as quickly as possible, him glowering at me for taking so long.

I hurried to the checkout as fast as I could with my items, the guard stuck to me like glue. The cashier seemed to catch the vibe because she checked me out quickly as well.

"The receipt's in the bag," she said as I took both my bags and started carrying them out the door. She gave the guard a look as though she was wondering why he didn't help me.

I figured it was because it would be harder to strangle me with his arms laden down with bananas and apples.

We got back in the car, and I saw from the clock on the dashboard that our little adventure took less than an hour. So much for fresh air.

Back in the apartment, I started to put away the groceries. My stomach rumbled, and I made myself a quick grilled cheese sandwich.

I felt like having a soda with it, so I took out one of the bottles I'd pulled cold from the case near the checkout. The receipt was stuck to it.

Not paying much attention, I peeled it off only to find it wasn't a receipt at all. At least, not now that it was wet with condensation.

'Darren's okay,' it read. 'Are you? We've hacked the camera feed to your apartment. Nod if you're okay.'

Startled, I nodded.

'Channel 567,' it said below that.

I abandoned my plated grilled cheese and my soda and went to the living room. I didn't know how they planned to make this communication work, given the presence of the cameras, but I was desperate, and if someone got into trouble for this, I wanted it to just be me. Not Caleb.

The remote shook in my hand as I turned on the TV and punched in channel 567.

There were a series of sounds all around the apartment as though things were powering down.

Darren came on the screen. "We don't have much time," he said. "As soon as they realize the cameras are down, they'll be in there to fix them. I just wanted to let you know we are still tracking you and are working on a plan to get you out. Let Caleb know, too."

I nodded, not trusting myself to speak.

The channel went to static, and I heard the keypad to the door begin to beep.

I quickly changed the channel to a light movie and went into the kitchen to gather up my soda and grilled cheese. I discreetly put the receipt in my pocket until it dried out or dissolved or did whatever it was going to do.

Two guards stormed inside the apartment, and I must have looked startled enough to pass muster because they grunted into their earpieces, "All clear."

"Is something wrong?" I asked.

"Nothing you need to worry about," one of the guards said. He went to the television and rather rudely turned off my movie so he could go to the channel for the cameras. One by one, they came back to life.

"False alarm," the other guard grumbled into his earpiece. "Looks like it was an internet glitch. They're coming back up now."

When all the cameras were back up, the guards left without a word.

I quietly microwaved my grilled cheese and went to watch my movie. I couldn't wait for Caleb to come home.

<hr>

CALEB RETURNED several hours later at about 7:00 PM looking haggard. I quickly set my pizza rolls aside and went over to him.

"Today I think I coordinated a mass kidnapping," he said to me when I went to hug him.

I hugged him anyway. "That's not your fault. That's Masterson's fault. He's just using you as a pawn."

"I know." Caleb hugged me tightly and buried his face in my hair. "I still feel evil, though."

I wrapped my arms around his neck and pressed my lips close to his ear. "I have good news," I breathed.

Caleb rubbed his hands up and down my back. "What news?" he whispered.

"Darren's okay, and they're trying to get us out," I murmured.

Caleb froze and looked down at me. "How do you know that?" he asked.

I put my lips back by his ear and explained the whole thing. I felt Caleb's chest heave against me as he took a strangled breath.

"Thank God," he whispered.

"So, I made pizza rolls. Want me to make some more for y—?" My words ended on a squeal as Caleb picked me up and slung me over his shoulder.

"Later. I'm hungry for something else," he said. He swatted my ass as he carried me through the apartment and into the bedroom.

I bounced when I hit the mattress and laughed as Caleb took no time at all stripping off my pants and underwear. I wriggled out of my shirt and bra, and he stood and looked down at my body.

The urge to cover myself used to be strong, but now I just wanted to stoke his hunger, so I put my hands under my breasts as though offering them to him.

Caleb groaned and stripped his shirt off. He made short work of the rest of his clothes and got on the bed next to me, leaning on his side so his eyes could still eat me up unrestricted.

"I think you want me," I giggled.

"I think you're right," he grinned back.

"Then what are you doing?" I asked.

He winked at me. "Taking in the buffet."

I laughed. Then I groaned as he smoothed a hand up my belly and over my breast.

"You like that, baby?" Caleb asked.

"Very much," I admitted.

He followed the path of his hand with his lips, sucking at my nipples and neck. I knew he was giving me a hickey, and I didn't care.

"Marking your territory?" I gasped.

"Hell yes," he answered when his lips left my neck with a little pop. "I'm gonna plant my flag in a minute."

I giggled again. "You are so bad."

He smiled at me and kissed down my body this time. Caleb nudged my knees apart with his shoulders and licked his lips.

"Tonight, we feast!" he announced, and I laughed until I was moaning as he licked up inside me. I fisted my hands in his hair.

Caleb was not satisfied with just getting me wet and ready. He ate me out until I came against his mouth, calling out his name.

Then he did indeed 'plant his flag,' prowling up my body and pressing his lips to mine as he pushed his long, fat cock inside me.

I felt like we were celebrating. Like it was my birthday all over again. And I guessed we were celebrating. Darren was alive, and they were trying to get us out.

"You're still not wearing a condom," I pointed out on a gasp as Caleb started to thrust enthusiastically inside me.

"Did you get any from the grocery store?" he asked.

I knew I'd forgotten something. "No."

"Then I think we're just going to have to make peace with the fact that you're going to make me a daddy again," he said.

"You just like that I get all needy and randy," I muttered, going nearly cross-eyed at something Caleb did with his hips.

"That, too," Caleb admitted. He kept up the pace until I came with a cry. Then he thrust sharply twice more before he filled me up with his seed.

To my surprise, he kept going, making me orgasm again, then a fourth time, filling me up in between.

This was life-affirming sex. There was no other way to describe it. We had hope again, and we were sharing it and cementing it with our bodies.

We didn't stop until Caleb physically collapsed. He panted, lying on me while our slick bodies tried to catch up.

I wrapped my arms around his neck and played with the short hairs at the nape of his neck. Caleb kissed me long and slow, but there was nothing else to be done about it. We were both exhausted.

"Daddy's a little tired," I teased him.

"Daddy put in a full day of work," he reminded me. He did still give a half-hearted buck of his hips, but I rubbed my hands down his back, encouraging him to calm his body.

"We can do it again when you wake up," I said.

"We will, I promise you," he replied.

Caleb just managed to roll off of me before he settled into bed with a groan. "Must sleep."

"Probably a good idea," I agreed.

He patted his chest. "Need my blanket."

I reached down for the covers, but he grabbed my arm and pulled me across his chest instead. "Much better," he said.

Laughter filled the bedroom, followed by kissing, and then, finally, sleep.

"We're getting out of here," Caleb whispered just before he nodded off.

"We are," I said, my voice brimming with happiness.

HOPE SPRINGS ETERNAL

-Caleb-

I stroked Jacey's hair gently in the morning hours before I had to go work for the devil incarnate.

She stirred then snuggled into me more and tried to go back to sleep.

"Baby," I murmured, my hand moving down her back. "If we want to be together before I go to work, we have to start now."

Jacey grumbled and popped her head up off my shoulder. Her face was scrunched and adorable, so I kissed her nose.

"I love you," I said.

"Mmm, love you, too," she yawned.

I tickled the small of her back, and she giggled.

"It's not fair how much of a morning person you are," she sighed.

"It's not fair how beautiful you are in the morning, so I guess we're even," I replied.

Jacey scrunched up her nose again. "You, mister, are just trying to get laid."

"You know it," I grinned.

"You're incorrigible," she accused me.

"Absolutely and completely," I agreed. "So, are you going to hop aboard?" I stroked my length suggestively, showing her I was all warmed up and ready.

She rolled her eyes. "Work, work, work." Then she smiled at me, and it was like sunshine in my soul.

"Honestly, are you ready, or should we—?" I began.

Jacey straddled me and easily slid down onto my cock, making us both groan.

"Fuck," I grunted, putting my hands on her hips.

"Working on it," she teased in reply.

I growled, and together we got her riding me in a way that made us both happy. It was all I could do not to cum first.

"Baby, I'm close," I wheezed, thumbing her clit hard and fast.

She threw back her head and cried out, squeezing around my dick.

I came hard, giving her everything my balls had accumulated overnight.

Jacey dropped forward onto my chest. I wrapped my arms around her, still twitching inside her.

"Do you really have to go to work today?" she asked, hugging me.

"Mm-hmm," I responded. "You never know. Masterson might need me to have a small village wiped out so he can pillage a rainforest somewhere."

"Asshole," she sniffed, hugging me more tightly.

"That he is." I let myself lie in the carefree bliss of Jacey's warmth for a while, then I sighed and started to get up.

She made a sound of protest. "Stay."

"I'll be back later. Keep some pizza rolls warm for me." I rolled her underneath me and gently pulled out, then fingered her. "Or better yet, this. You can keep this warm for me."

"You need to eat," Jacey admonished me.

"I liked my dinner last night. Tasty." I licked my lips.

"I mean real food," she huffed.

I shrugged. "We'll see what we're in the mood for when I get home."

We both made a face. Starting to think of this apartment as home was disturbing on so many levels.

"I'll see you later, okay?" I said, rapidly glossing over my last statement. I pulled my fingers out of her and went to get dressed.

"Okay." Jacey got up and helped me pick out a tie.

After I was dressed, we kissed again by the front door, and my two guards escorted me away.

I decided I'd better keep an eye out in case Darren tried to contact us again in some unexpected way.

The car ride to the office was uneventful. I paused by the entrance, half wondering if Darren would be there again, inviting me to coffee.

But the only people who were watching for me were my guards.

"Got something in your teeth?" one asked as I paused by the glass doors into the building.

"No, sorry. Daydreaming," I replied, shaking myself.

The guards both snickered. "Man, if my woman gave me sex like that, I'd be daydreaming all the time," the second one said.

I scowled at him but didn't comment. I took the elevator to the executive floor and reported to my desk, as usual.

Masterson came out of his office to torment me. "I think there's a village in Brazil that needs clearing before we can pillage their resources," he chuckled to me.

Doubtless he'd been listening to our conversation last night. I hadn't meant to give him ideas. "Can we not? I mean, doesn't your legitimate business make enough money?" I asked in a low tone.

"There's never enough money, Caleb," Masterson said.

"I feel sad for you, then," I responded.

Masterson's expression turned sour. "Don't you dare pity me, boy."

"It's not exactly something I have control over," I said.

"Just fucking do your job," Masterson growled. He shoved a sheaf of papers at me.

I went to my desk and sat down, shaking my head. Masterson was a real piece of work. I opened my desk to get my staple remover when I heard a crackle.

Confused, I felt under the drawer and came up with a Post-It note.

'We are watching,' it said.

I didn't know if this was a threat from Masterson or a note of comfort from Darren. Which meant I didn't know whether to be relieved or intimidated. Either way, I wanted to get rid of it, so I scribbled the words away with a pen and dropped the note in my trash.

The rest of my day was spent talking to a mercenary group for hire about 'cleansing' a village of about a hundred people from the Amazon Rainforest so that Masterson could send in his team to go divest the land of its protected trees. It was a protected tribe of indigenous people with few left in the world, and I was arranging to mow down half of those who were left.

Instead of eating lunch, I threw up in the bathroom.

"How's it going in there?" one of my guards chuckled. They were enjoying the hell out of my torment.

"Fine," I urped. Then I dry heaved.

I heard a tapping sound and looked up to see a vent. Sticking out of it was one of those cameras that were popular in action movies-a long, black snake thing.

"Seriously?" I grumbled.

There was a crackle, then the speaker over my head stopped playing soothing elevator music. "We're coming soon," I heard a soft whisper.

Then the music returned. I almost thought I'd hallucinated in my food-deprived state. But I held on to the idea I hadn't hallucinated, and Darren really was coming. That knowledge got me out of the bathroom and back into the office.

"Eat something that didn't agree with you?" Masterson asked sweetly.

"I guess so," I replied with nearly as much cheer. Someday, I was going to nail this fucker's ass to the wall. Jacey and me both.

Masterson's eyes narrowed, but luckily he decided I was just messing with him and went back into his office.

I went back to tracking people in shipping containers and asking underage sex trafficking rings for their expense reports.

The day dragged on and on. More than anything, I wanted to give

Masterson the finger and leave, confident that Darren would be there to scoop me up. But I didn't know any of that for sure, so I did what I supposed Darren wanted me to do. I sat tight.

"You're just a busy bee," Lacy said toward the end of the day when she came out of Masterson's office, buttoning her shirt. "I've never seen you this focused!"

I grimaced. "Yes, well, someone's gotta do it."

"True. Hey, you, Jacey, and I should go out for drinks," Lacy suggested.

I raised an eyebrow at her. "I don't know how that would work. And Jacey's not old enough to drink."

"Oh. Wow, you do like them young," Lacy grinned.

"I'm twenty-three," I reminded her.

"Lord, you're just barely old enough to drink yourself. All right, we'll have to do dinner or coffee or something. I miss her," Lacy said. "She was fun to work with."

It boggled my mind how Lacy just rolled with everything. Like this was a normal workplace, and Masterson hadn't tried to rape my girlfriend. "Yeah, I'm sure she was," I responded, bemused.

"Anyway, I should get back to reception. I'll catch you later!" Lacy smiled and wandered off.

I stared after her, trying to think of what could have possessed her to be so bubbly when it was obvious I was there against my will.

When I returned to my desk, there was a nondescript envelope on it. My stomach tightened, and I sat down and quickly opened it, trying to be discreet.

'Parking Garage,' was all it said.

I hoped whoever it was meant they'd be doing whatever they were planning once I got there at the end of the day because there was no way I could sneak there now.

The whole rest of the day was a blur. I worried about how they were going to get Jacey out. I wondered what would happen if they got me and not her. A thousand catastrophic scenarios swirled in my mind.

When it was finally time to go back to the apartment, my two guards flanked me and brought me to the elevators. My stomach knotted painfully while we descended to the garage level.

"Just be glad the boss didn't want you catching a cold in the rain. Otherwise, we'd be doing a pick-up outside," one of my guards grunted.

"I kind of figured," I managed.

The elevator stopped.

"Get down," my other guard said to me.

I was confused for the heartbeat it took for the first guard to turn to the second. "What?" he said.

The second guard took out a gun, and I hit the floor.

When the elevator doors opened, Darren was there with five other agents.

"You coming with us?" the second guard asked the first in a bored tone.

"Not on your life," the first guard snorted.

"Pity." The second guard smacked the first across the back of the head, downing him.

"Let's go, Caleb," Darren said.

I got up and took Darren's hand. He and the other agents rushed me into an SUV that came tearing up.

Jacey was not inside.

"Darren, where's Jacey?" I asked worriedly.

"She's meeting us at our next destination. Okay, Travis, go, go, GO!" Darren said.

I just managed to get my seatbelt on before we went careening through the parking garage. Travis held a gun on the parking attendant when we reached the exit. "This the hill you want to die on?" he asked.

The attendant prudently let us out.

Four other black SUVs of the exact same make and model met us on the street.

"Clothes," Darren said. "You never know where they might have put a tracker."

I stripped as quickly as I had in my life, and Darren dropped everything out the window before handing me a tracksuit.

The other SUVs kept pace with us, despite the flying clothes. We moved as a unit for a while then branched off in five different directions.

"Let him try and figure that one out," Darren crowed.

"Is Jacey in one of those?" I asked.

"No. There's a different plan to get her. It was a simultaneous thing, though, so she should be arriving at our destination at the same time we do," Darren said.

"Should be?" I echoed.

Darren sighed. "I can't predict everything, Caleb. All we can do is try our best."

I sat back with a swallow. There was nothing I could do now but pray.

-Jacey-

It was when the smoke detector went off that I realized something was wrong.

I sat up in bed and blinked at the darkness. Caleb wasn't home yet, and I'd decided to take a little nap before he arrived just in case he was in the mood for rigorous after dinner activities.

Confused, I went to the door, but the handle was hot. My third grade fire safety knowledge came rushing back to me all at once, and I knew not to open the door. Smoke began pouring up from under the bottom of the door, however. Panicking, I reached for one of Caleb's sweaters and rolled it up on the carpet to block the incoming smoke.

Then I backed to the window. I tried to open it, thinking I could at least get the smoke out of the room and maybe be in position if a firefighter came up looking for me. But the window wouldn't budge. I realized, belatedly, it was nailed shut. Apparently Mr. Masterson hadn't wanted either Caleb or me pulling a Spiderman and trying to crawl along the building ledge to another residence.

This left me well and truly trapped.

Over the crackle of flames and creak of things being consumed and weakened by fire, I heard yelling.

"Fuck, we have to go in and get her!" I recognized one of my guards' voices.

"Fuck that, man. I don't get paid enough to be barbecued. You want to go get her? You go right ahead. I'm outta here," the other guard said.

There was a pause, then the first guard agreed. "Whatever. She's probably dead already anyway."

I realized then I was on my own. "Oh God."

My third grade happy skit about fire safety did not cover this. What if no one came? What if the firefighters couldn't get to me?!

I looked at the closed windows and picked up a chair, beating it against the glass. But it bounced right off as though it were bullet-proof or something.

"Help!" I called, pounding my fists on the window. I tried turning the light on in the bedroom, but the wires must have melted or something because nothing happened. "Please."

Smoke began filtering into the room despite the sweater, around the edges of the door, and I plastered myself to the wall, trying to stay away from it.

I was so focused on the smoke that I didn't see the man in black until he knocked on my window.

Jumping, I turned to look. The man was on nylon rappelling rope and was dressed entirely in black, including the mask over his face.

He looked more like a thief than a rescuer, but I wasn't going to be a choosy beggar. The man waved for me to move away from the window.

I skirted along the wall as far away as the opposite wall would let me.

The man stuck something squishy to the window, then moved away himself. There was a loud pop, and then the window shattered.

"Come on," he said, gesturing me over to the exploded window.

As we were on the seventh floor, I knew I was going to have to be brave. I pulled on a pair of tennis shoes, then ran over in my pajamas

—consisting of Caleb's boxers and a T-shirt—and held out my arms to my savior.

He pulled me up onto the windowsill, which was not ideal, given the glass, and quickly hooked me into a harness connected to his. "Hang on," he ordered.

I wrapped myself around his torso, and we went rappelling down the building. I squeezed my eyes shut so I wouldn't do anything stupid like scream. This seemed like Darren's plans at work, and I didn't want to ruin them by drawing attention to us.

"You're a very brave girl," the man said when we finally hit the pavement. He unclipped me, then detached himself from the rope and dragged me into the alley around the back of the building.

At one end, a black sedan was waiting.

"Get in and go. Go!" he told me, giving me a push in that direction.

I scrambled through the alley and launched myself into the sedan, my head bumping someone's thigh. Given that thigh was wearing expensive pants, I began to worry that I was being tricked and had just gone through this whole ordeal only to find Masterson was playing another one of his sick games.

However, when I looked up, I saw Jake, the guy from the funeral.

"Hi," he said, his expression as bewildered as I felt.

"Hi," I replied.

"So, apparently Masterson wants to kill me. I'm getting the impression he's not terribly fond of you," Jake said.

"You'd be right." We both swayed as the sedan took off, careening through the streets of Minneapolis until we hit the highway and became just another nondescript vehicle in the Minnesota night.

The partition was up between us and whoever was driving, so it was impossible to see exactly who was taking us where.

"Were you picked up by the FBI?" I asked.

"Yeah. You?" Jake replied.

"I'm guessing so? We didn't have a lot of time for introductions," I explained.

"From the way the fire engines were racing to the building, and how scuffed up your legs are, I kind of got that impression," Jake said.

I looked down at my legs and winced. "I suppose I should make sure I don't have glass stuck in any of this mess."

"Sometimes you're not supposed to pull it out," Jake warned.

"I'll be careful." I sat up and began picking at my legs. Luckily, there wasn't a lot of glass at all.

Jake handed me a handkerchief to put the few pieces of glass there were into it. I disposed of the glass, then set the handkerchief aside. "Thanks."

"You're welcome." Jake was about to say something else, but then we skidded to a stop, making both of us roll forward and knock our heads on the partition.

"Ouch," Jake groaned.

The door on Jake's side opened, and I recognized one of my day guards. "Jake, no! Don't go with him! He's—!"

"Very good at keeping secrets," the day guard winked and pulled out a badge, tossing it to me. "You have no idea what a pain in the ass it was to work for Masterson all this time. Or maybe you would."

"Oh my God, you could have told me!" I huffed, tossing his badge back at him.

The FBI agent caught it in the air. "You don't do that when you're undercover. Six years. Finally get to go home and see my family."

"Where are we?" Jake asked.

"We're at your safe house, kid. I'm taking Jacey here to a different one," the FBI agent said. "Darren will be by soon to see if there's any useful information you have about Masterson, but we know she has some so we've got to get her off and prepped."

"Will there be a trial soon?" I responded hopefully.

"It'll still be a while. Compiling all the evidence and everything. But this time, we're not letting you out of our sight," the FBI agent said. "Now, come on out, Jake. We've got to get you tucked away so I can take Jacey where she needs to go."

Jake got out of the car and followed the FBI agent in the direction of a house I saw just in the distance. Only they veered off to the right suddenly.

"What…?" I murmured, getting out of the car myself and tiptoeing after them.

"What did I do?" I could hear Jake babbling. "Tell me what I did!"

"You ruined Mr. Masterson's funeral," the FBI agent said flatly as I approached. I saw, as I peeked my head out from behind a tree, that he was holding a gun in the moonlight.

To Jake's credit, he lifted his chin and gave the FBI agent a derisive look. "It was Will's funeral."

"Yeah, you let that comfort you on your way to hell." The FBI agent put the gun to Jake's temple.

"I'll see you there," Jake replied.

I screamed. "NO!!!"

The FBI agent turned, and Jake took the opportunity to grab for the gun. A shot went off and Jake groaned.

"Fucking hell," the FBI agent said. He turned and pointed the gun in my direction while Jake curled on the ground, holding his stomach.

I turned and ran.

Another shot went off, and a bullet clipped my arm, spinning me around and making me slam into a tree.

The FBI agent loomed over me moments later. "You're lucky Masterson wants you alive."

I gripped my arm, my head spinning from colliding with the tree, and began to back away.

"Where do you think you're going?" the FBI agent snickered. "It's not like there's anywhere out here for you to go. That house? Masterson's."

Not willing to give up, I continued backing away.

The FBI agent moved forward like lightning and gripped my shirt. "You don't learn, do you?"

"And you're an idiot, Nelson," Darren's familiar voice snapped. I turned to see his gun leveled on Nelson, and five other agents with him. "Or did you forget our cars have GPS tracking?"

Nelson pushed me in front of him. "You won't risk her life."

"You're right." Darren cocked his head.

There was a loud shot behind us, and then Nelson crumpled to the ground.

"Darren," I choked, going to him. He tucked me into his side. "Darren, you have to go help Jake."

"We've got paramedics there already. Don't worry." Darren's jaw worked as he looked down at Nelson's dead body. "Traitor."

I shuddered. "Can you take me to Caleb?"

"Most certainly." Darren kept his arm around me and walked me away from the terrible scene. I knew Nelson's sightless eyes would haunt me until the day I died.

"She needs to be checked out, too. It looks like one of those bullets grazed her, and she's got a nice goose egg starting on her forehead," one of the other agents said, holstering his weapon.

"I don't trust hospitals right now. Have Wade come to the safe house with a kit. I think she's okay, and I want to know if we absolutely have to take her in," Darren replied. He looked over my head in the direction of the house and scowled. "That bastard."

I followed his line of sight and saw Mr. Masterson standing at the house's tall windows, staring at all the activity out on his property. We were just close enough to see him smirk and raise a glass, toasting us.

"Permission to ram that single-malt scotch right up his ass, sir?" one of Darren's agents asked.

"We've got him now. There's no wiggling out of this one." Darren raised a middle finger back at Mr. Masterson.

"Come on, boss. Let's get her to the real safe house," another agent said, corralling Darren and me and herding us toward the dark SUVs parked out on the street. He gave a cursory glance at my injuries. "Bullet wound's just a graze. You are going to want Wade to check her for a concussion."

"Noted."

Darren sat next to me as we drove all through the rest of the night. In the morning, we came upon a cottage by a lake and the SUV entourage stopped.

"Caleb's in there," Darren informed me. "Is Wade here?"

"He's waiting inside," another agent said.

We got out of the SUV and walked up to the cottage. The door burst open and a frantic-looking Caleb came bolting out. "Jacey, are you okay?! What's all this blood?!"

"I'll tell you in a bit, Caleb. I have to see a doctor now. Or a medic or somebody," I replied, trying with my tone to calm him down.

Caleb wasn't having it. "Why does she look like she's been through a war zone?"

"Masterson," Darren grunted.

It was all he needed to say. "I'm going to kill him," Caleb said.

ANOTHER LAKE

-Caleb-

Wade was not my favorite person right now.

As he laid Jacey carefully down on the sofa and checked for even pupil dilation, I paced the rug anxiously.

"Sit down, Caleb," Darren said after a while.

"She's fine. Maybe a very mild concussion, but she shouldn't need to see a doctor," Wade muttered, putting his penlight away. He got out a needle and some thread-like substance. "Dissolving stitches," he explained to me when I opened my mouth to ask. He concentrated on Jacey's grazed arm, carefully sewing the wound shut.

"Look at her legs! What the hell happened?!" I demanded to know.

Jacey, Darren, and Wade all looked at me with failing patience on their faces. "They did get me out, Caleb," she said.

"Yes, but look at you! You got shot!" I gestured at her arm.

"He was a bad agent. I'm sure we've run into a few before," she sighed.

I snapped my attention to Darren. "A rogue agent shot my Jacey?!"

"It never occurred to me that he could be bought," Darren said sadly. "I thought he was a good agent."

"Well, obviously not. He shot Jacey!" I pointed out.

Darren nodded solemnly. "Obviously not."

"Caleb, it happened. And I'm getting treated. It's all okay now. We're together," Jacey said, reaching for my hand.

I went over and knelt beside the chair, taking her hand. "I won't feel okay until Masterson is in prison. Maybe in hell."

"Believe me, we've been tempted," Wade muttered. "But we're the good guys, and the good guys don't just go around shooting people."

"That's unfortunate," I grumbled.

"Some days, it is," Darren agreed.

Jacey looked over at Darren. "How long do we get to stay here?"

"Hopefully, for the duration. I'm taking the bedroom down the hall, and there will be round the clock agents guarding the property. He's going to have a lot more trouble snatching you next time, if he tries," Darren said.

"More trouble? Can't we just go somewhere where it would be impossible?" I asked.

"Nothing's impossible, Caleb," Darren sighed. "This is the absolute best we can do."

"Great." I grimaced but Jacey squeezed my hand.

"They're doing their best, Caleb. You could still be in a Canadian prison, you know," she reminded me.

I took her meaning and gave in with a long breath. "I wish the trial was happening tomorrow."

"Don't we all. But the law moves slowly, and we really want to nail this slippery bastard to the wall," Wade said. "So that means even more slowly."

Jacey squeezed my hand again when I groaned. "I think maybe it would be a good idea to get me an IUD, if that's possible," she requested softly. "If I'm not already pregnant."

Darren and Wade stared at us.

"Honestly, Caleb, she's nineteen years old. Don't you ever learn?!" Darren yelled.

I winced. "He didn't exactly provide us with condoms."

"It would have killed you to keep it in your pants?" Darren scowled at me.

"It probably would have, yes," I replied honestly.

Darren shook his head. "I don't suppose you have any pregnancy tests with you, do you Wade?"

Wade rummaged in his duffel and pulled out two. "As soon as I finish here, you need to go pee on a stick," he said to Jacey.

She nodded, her cheeks flushed with embarrassment.

"I don't suppose anyone's ever made you sleep in the same space as your wife and expected you to keep your hands to yourself," I grunted at Darren.

"You couldn't have maybe taken the couch?" Darren suggested.

"Masterson likes to watch," Jacey informed them. "If we didn't perform, he might have separated us for good." She bit her lip. "How is Will Jr.? Do you know?"

Darren looked pained. "He's fine. Just living with the devil incarnate."

"Oh. Yeah, just that." She looked sad.

"All finished," Wade said. "Off to the bathroom with you."

I went with Jacey, but she shooed me out of the bathroom when I would have gone in with her. "Just give me a few seconds. Then you can come in."

About two minutes later, Jacey called out, "Okay, you can come watch the lines with me!"

I walked into the bathroom and sat on the edge of the bathtub while Jacey sat on the toilet. We watched patiently for several minutes. Just one line appeared.

"Okay, we're not pregnant," I said, though I felt a little sad about that.

"No, we're not." She sounded both sad and relieved at the same time.

"Do you suppose Wade can place an IUD? We both know how I am with condoms." I winced.

"Yeah, we should go see what Wade can do," she said.

We wandered out of the bathroom with the negative pregnancy tests. Darren sagged with relief, and Wade nodded. "Good. No extra problems," he commented.

"What do we do about getting Jacey an IUD?" I asked.

"Because you're too important to wear a condom?" Darren snorted.

"No. Because I forget. We both do. We get caught up in the moment, and I just want to make sure the necessary precautions are taken," I replied patiently.

"We'll get a gynecological team in here as soon as possible," Darren said. "I want them to give Jacey a proper physical anyway after having Will Jr. I don't trust Masterson as far as I can throw him."

"He had a private doctor taking care of her, but I like that idea," I responded.

Jacey's face scrunched up.

"What?" Darren asked.

"He killed the doctor," she said. "Shot him because he couldn't save Will when he committed suicide."

"Any idea where the body is buried?" Wade asked.

She shook her head. "I was in the trunk of the car with the body. Then we stopped in the woods, and they buried him before taking me to Caleb. I couldn't see my exact surroundings."

"Damn. I'm sorry you had to experience that," Darren said.

She shrugged. "It's just another thing on the list of awful things that man has done or has allowed to be done."

"Or has actively orchestrated," I grumbled. "He's a very, very bad man."

"What did he have you do now?" Daren asked.

"Track people in shipping containers. Organize the wiping out of a village in Brazil so he can do some illegal logging in the rainforest there. You know. Just the fun stuff," I snarked. "I have to say, the highlight was listening to someone get killed over the phone when a human trafficking shipment went bad. He had them all slaughtered."

Darren nodded. "It's good you overheard all that."

"Overheard? Hell, I *did* some of it. He still has our parents—oh my God, our parents!" I gaped.

"We'll do our best for them. As far as I know, they are still at Masterson's estate with your brother, Timothy," Darren said.

"You have to get them out of there, otherwise we can't testify. He'll kill someone!" I argued.

Wade snickered. "Oh, boy, you have a lot to learn about the legal system, kid."

"What?" I asked. "What does the legal system have to do with our parents and our brother being in danger?"

"You just admitted to actively participating in several crimes. If you don't want to go to prison, you're going to testify," Wade responded harshly.

I blinked. "What?"

"What Wade is failing to put delicately is that you need to testify if we're going to get you any kind of immunity for what you've done," Darren rephrased.

"Just what part of 'we were kidnapped and held hostage and threatened with death and the death of our loved ones' did you fail to understand?!" I shouted.

Jacey was pale, but she took my hand between hers and rubbed the back of my hand soothingly with her thumb. "We'll testify, Darren."

"But, Jacey, Hank and Mom and Timothy—" I argued.

"Are not going to be helped by us staying quiet. We have to testify, or this is never going to end, Caleb," she said softly.

I frowned, but she did have a point. "What about our parents and Timothy?" I asked.

"What is he going to do to them that he wouldn't do anyway?" Her voice was thick with defeat.

"So we give up? Leave them for dead?" I shot back.

Jacey burst into tears, and I instantly regretted my words. "I'm sorry," I said. "I'm sorry, baby, I didn't mean it."

"Charming." Wade finished putting his things away. "Well, at least we don't need to worry about any accidental pregnancies until the gyno team gets here. He'll be lucky if she doesn't cut his dick off for that one."

"Caleb, Jacey, I know you're both under a lot of stress," Darren sighed. "But I need you to not break team. You've been doing so well so far."

Jacey dropped my hand and ran from the room.

"Caleb, has anyone told you recently that you're an idiot?" Darren asked, shaking his head.

"I'll fix it." I got up and went after Jacey.

She'd gone out the back door, down to the dock, and was standing over the lake. I made my way down to stand beside her. "I wasn't saying you were giving up," I tried to explain. "I was saying they were. What can we do to help them, anyway? Darren says he's going to try his best, but we've seen where his best got us before. I don't want that to happen to our family."

Jacey was silent. She wouldn't look at me.

"Baby, I mean it; I wasn't yelling at you," I said brokenly. "Please don't ice me out."

She looked up, and her eyes were red with tears. And I'd put them there.

I reached for her, but she took a step back. My heart broke. "Jacey?"

"You're sleeping on the sofa until the gynecologist comes," she informed me hollowly. "After that, we can talk. But don't you touch me, Caleb Killeen. Don't you touch me right now."

She headed back up to the house.

I crumpled down and sat at the edge of the dock, feeling rejected and useless. And it was my own damn fault.

Darren came down about half an hour later as I was watching the sunset. "Couples fight sometimes, son. It happens."

Subtly, I rubbed my eyes then looked up at Darren. "Yeah?"

"Usually because a guy was a dumbass. But, there you have it. It'll blow over or you'll talk it out. You're going to be okay," Darren assured me.

"What if she doesn't want to work it out?" I whispered.

"That girl looks at you like the sun shines out of your ass. Trust me. You'll work it out," Darren said.

"Is she okay? Where did she go?" I asked.

Darren pointed to one side of the house. "She's in the bedroom, crying her eyes out. You've got to let her have that."

"I don't want her crying her eyes out just because I was a dumbass," I said.

"It's not your choice. The sofa pulls out into a bed. I made it up for you." Darren looked out at the water.

"She doesn't want to talk about things until the gyno's been here. When will that be?" I asked.

He blew out a long breath. "About a week."

"A week?! But she could hate me by then!" I gasped. "No, come on. There has to be, like, some emergency gyno or something. Somebody. Anybody."

"Caleb, you're just going to have to grin and bear it for now," he said. "This is the best I can do."

I punched a dock post, which wasn't the greatest idea. My knuckles split, and my hand throbbed. "I'm so damned tired of hearing how people are doing their best."

"It's the truth. You'd rather I lie to you?" Darren asked.

"No." I hung my head, feeling helpless.

He clapped me on the shoulder. "Come on. Let's get you settled. I think making some food might go a long way."

"You think she'll eat with me?" I replied hopefully.

"No, but I think if you set a tray outside her door, she'll appreciate it," Darren said.

I got up and walked back to the house with Darren. He gave me a tour of where everything in the kitchen was then left me there to cook.

Remembering he was staying with us, I made three grilled cheese sandwiches.

FORGIVENESS

-Jacey-

I spent most of the evening crying into my pillow. How could Caleb have said that? He made it sound as though I didn't care about our family at all.

The only times I left my bed were to go to the bathroom. Luckily, I had an en suite, so I didn't have to go out into the hall and risk running into Caleb.

At some point, I heard a scraping sound near my door, but Caleb did not try to knock or come inside. I wasn't sure if I was relieved or disappointed.

I crept to my door and opened it. No one was there. I was just about to close the door when I saw a food tray lying on the floor.

Grilled cheese, a glass of milk, some potato chips, and carrot sticks.

Tears welled in my eyes again and I picked up the tray and went into the bedroom, closing the door with my foot.

I sat on the bed and ate, sniffling between bites. When I went to dab my mouth with a napkin, I saw Caleb had written something on the other side.

I switched on my bedside lamp and held the napkin under it to read Caleb's sloppy handwriting.

Jacey,

Darren says I should leave you alone, but I just wanted you to know I love you and I'm ready to talk when you are.

Come out when you're ready.

Love,

Caleb

More tears rolled down my cheeks and smudged the writing on the napkin. I left it on the bedside dresser and set my empty tray on a chair.

Caleb had made dinner for me even though I was icing him out. It was probably the sweetest thing I could think of.

I curled up on the bed, thinking about what Caleb had said and going over our conversation after. I knew he wouldn't deliberately accuse me of not caring. I just wondered if he felt I didn't and it slipped out sideways.

I didn't think I could bear it if Caleb thought I was some sort of monster.

Crunching myself into a tight ball, I knotted my hands together and started to pray. I prayed for my family, Dad, Timothy, and even Jeanie. I also prayed for Jake, who I hadn't seen again. I prayed for Will Jr. and his father, Will, hoping Will was in a better place. And then I prayed that Caleb really did still love me.

It wasn't going to get any easier finding out if I hid in my room. Did I have the courage to go out, knowing this coming conversation with Caleb might be the end?

If we talked, and he realized while we were talking that he didn't love me anymore, I would be crushed. I would never recover. I knew it sounded like something every lovesick nineteen-year-old might say. That they'd never get over their teenage crush. But in this case it was true. Caleb was all I had now. What would I do without him?

And how would we live here, together, and not be in love? We'd be waiting, what, a year for the trial? Would it be better to live here with him knowing he'd never love me back again or would the FBI separate us? Would it be better or worse if we were separated?

I realized then that I'd convinced myself I could survive anything as long as I had Caleb. What would happen if I didn't have him anymore?

All I could imagine was a gaping hole in my heart, large enough to swallow me up. I'd had hopes before Caleb. Dreams. Plans. Then the situation with Masterson happened, and all that went away. I should be in college right now, sneaking around with my older boyfriend, reading my homework on my tablet while he laid his head in my lap in a beat up dorm room too small for two people.

I'd always imagined Caleb would be that boyfriend. And he'd cheer me on in my studies and celebrate my accomplishments with me. He'd be busy as hell himself with medical school.

Masterson had denied us that opportunity. For a while, he'd even denied us each other, getting me pregnant with Will's son while Caleb was forced to stay in a bedroom on the estate by himself. It nearly killed him then.

It nearly killed me.

What if we weren't those people once we were out of danger? We hadn't had a chance to grow together organically as we should have. Everything was always danger, danger, danger!

Who was I without Caleb?

I needed to figure that out before I had any more conversations with him about our future. It wasn't fair to me or to him to not know the answer to that question. I wasn't naive enough to think two people became one person when they merged their lives. They were still two people who consciously decided to build their lives together, knowing each one was going to grow and change and willing to go along for the journey anyway.

If I couldn't be my own person in this relationship, that was a problem. I wasn't just some barnacle clinging to Caleb. At least, I hoped I wasn't.

I lay on my back and stared at the ceiling. When we put Masterson in prison and this was all over, what did I want?

I knew I wanted to go to college. That much I knew I wanted for myself. I'd also like to have a family with Caleb. But... did I really want that now?

There was some choice in the matter. I was getting that IUD so Caleb and I could make love without worrying about me getting pregnant. But I also had Will Jr. to think about. If Masterson went to prison, would they give him to me? I hoped so.

Was it fair to wrangle Caleb into that situation? Will Jr. technically wasn't his, even though he'd promised to be a good father to him. Caleb wanted to go to medical school. Would it even be possible for me to go to college and Caleb to go to medical school with a toddler?

I reminded myself that other people made it work.

So many questions. I contemplated them late into the night. I had no idea where we were, if we were in Minnesota, or another state, or back in Canada. But the stars came out here, bright, away from the city lights. I counted them, wishing on each one that this situation would come to a happy ending.

There was a soft knock at my door, and I went to answer it. A ragged-looking Caleb stood there, his head slightly bowed as though he was ashamed.

"I can't sleep," he said softly. "Isn't that something? I don't know how to sleep without you anymore."

After a few moments of silence to think it over, I took Caleb's hand and tugged him into my room. "Come to bed," I whispered.

Caleb stepped inside the bedroom, then pulled me against him, hugging me tightly. "Jacey, please don't be mad at me anymore. I'm sorry."

"I know," I said. I touched the side of his face, looked deep into his wounded eyes, then kissed him.

Caleb groaned and closed the door with his foot. He backed me to the bed, and we tumbled over onto it together.

I could feel how much he wanted me against my thigh. He came up from the kiss with a gasp and framed my face with his hands.

"Let me?" he asked. "Please? I need to be inside you."

"I don't know if there are condoms in here," I replied hesitantly.

Caleb leaned up and opened the bedside dresser drawer. He cursed. "They're the wrong size."

"Too small?" I guessed.

"Too small," Caleb sighed. He sat up and scrubbed his scruffy chin, his eyes hot on me. I was still wearing a T-shirt and his boxers from earlier, but he looked at me as though he could see right through them.

"I don't think we should get pregnant right now, Caleb. I love you so much. But I love you enough to want you to do all the things you always wanted. Like medical school," I said softly.

He lay down beside me, brushing the hair off my cheek. "You've been crying."

"Yeah," I admitted.

Caleb kissed my tear trails. "It's my fault."

"Not totally. I've been thinking," I responded.

"That's never a good sign," he winced.

"Am I holding you back, Caleb? When all this is over, I'll probably have a toddler—"

"We," he said. "We will have a toddler. I promised you, and I promised Will. That boy is my son, no matter what."

Tears pricked my eyes. "But what if we don't stay together?"

Caleb stiffened. "Then we'll have shared custody, I suppose. But I'm still convinced *we* are a good idea. Aren't you?"

"Yes," I choked. I wrapped myself around him. "I think we're the best idea since the creation of the universe."

"Good." Caleb sounded relieved.

"I love you," I said, kissing his neck. "I just don't want to be a burden. I'm a whole person. I don't want you to have to take care of me when you have dreams of your own."

"That's too bad because I'm going to take care of you. And you're going to take care of me. You're my biggest dream, Jacey. Don't ever forget that," Caleb replied, hugging me fiercely.

I burst into tears. "I feel the same way about you, Caleb."

"Then let's not talk about not being together ever again," he murmured into my hair. "Because I swear, Jacey, if we get through, all this and you break up with me, it will kill me."

"Me, too," I breathed.

Caleb kissed me, his own tears mingling with mine. I felt his hard length against me and knew we both needed to connect. It was more important than anything else.

I wriggled out of Caleb's boxers and reached into his sweatpants.

He groaned when I freed his dick. "Jacey, what about…?"

"Hush," I said. "Nothing else matters right now." I threw one leg over his hip then guided the fat head of his cock to my opening.

Caleb moaned and sank inside. No condoms. No barriers. Just us and this overwhelming need to be together.

I clung to his shoulders as he gripped my ass cheeks and started to thrust.

"You are the best thing that ever happened to me, Jacey. Don't ever doubt it," he murmured while punctuating each word with another thrust.

I couldn't speak. The pleasure had built up too much. I just whimpered against his lips.

"Don't worry, baby. I'm going to take you there," Caleb said, and just as the first hot jet of his cum began to fill me up, I went right over the edge and cried out, digging my nails into his shoulders,

He hissed and kept cumming, pumping his cock in and out as he twitched inside me. He stayed rigid with need, even when he finished, and touched my cheek. "Baby…"

I pressed my lips to his. "Keep going, love."

Caleb rolled me onto my back and encouraged me to lock my legs around his waist. He pulled my top over my head, then his own, then kissed each of my palms before putting them over his nipples. I rubbed him there, and his cock got even more swollen inside me.

He undulated his hips against mine, thrusting powerfully, his hands at my waist, his eyes eating up the scene of my breasts bouncing.

I thumbed his nipples and his eyelids fluttered.

"Damn, baby, you feel so good," he sighed. He moved his thumb from my waist to my clit and rubbed me there while he thrust.

I panted and felt myself at the razor's edge of orgasm.

Then Caleb leaned down and whispered in my ear, "Make me a daddy again, baby."

That did it. I was completely undone, coming hard around his cock, sobbing and nodding and tightening my legs around his waist so he could be as deep in me as possible when he gave me his seed.

He kissed me and came, panting, pressing his forehead to mine. "No IUD."

I swallowed and shook my head. "No IUD."

Caleb put a hand over my stomach. "I'm gonna put a baby in here."

"Yes," I agreed.

"And after that one, I'm putting another one in here," Caleb informed me.

I laughed weakly. "How many do you want?"

"As many as you'll bless me with," he said and kissed me again.

UNPOPULAR DECISIONS

-Caleb-

"You've decided what now?" Darren gaped.

"We're going to get pregnant," I replied. "So, please have the gyno come to make sure she's well, but…"

"… I won't be needing an IUD," Jacey said, leaning her head against my shoulder.

Darren closed his eyes, his lips moving as though he was counting to ten. Maybe a hundred. "You're just kids. Jacey, you're nineteen. And you're in witness protection. I think it might be best if you waited."

"We feel differently," I insisted. "I mean, we're going to be in witness protection forever, right?"

Darren gave me a look. "I'm talking to Jacey."

I looked down at her, feeling bad for talking over her. "Sorry."

She patted my arm reassuringly. "I want to start having a family. I want to start my life."

"Yes, but eventually, even though you'll still be in witness protection, you'll be able to go to college. That's going to be hard," Darren said.

"By that time, we'll have Will Jr. anyway. He is my son," she reminded him.

Darren stroked his chin. "I suppose that's true. But two kids is going to be even more challenging."

"We want to try," Jacey said.

He threw up his hands. "Ugh. You two are going to be the death of me. Fine, fine, I'll get the gyno here, and we'll make sure you're healthy after your ordeal. Healthy enough to have more kids."

She went and hugged him. "Thanks, Darren."

"Also, the condoms were too small, anyway," I added.

Darren snorted. "All men say that."

"It's true," Jacey confirmed. "Caleb's… um… big."

I smirked at Darren.

"I suppose that's one thing you have going for you," he muttered.

"I'm going to medical school when this is all over, so I'm going to be more than just a big dick," I defend myself.

His expression turned to surprise and then discomfort. "Caleb… you can't go to medical school."

"What?" I said.

"They'll be looking for you to do just that after the trial is over. You have to choose a different profession," Darren explained.

I tensed, and Jacey grabbed my arm, no doubt thinking I was going to take a swing at him. "But I've been studying pre-med."

"I'm sorry." He shook his head. "I truly am sorry, Caleb, but it's just not possible. You're a fine executive assistant. Maybe you'd like to go into business for yourself or sell real estate or any number of other options. You just can't go to medical school."

"Fuck." I felt angry, sick, and disappointed at the same time. I wanted to scream. I wanted to tear out Masterson's throat with my bare hands. "That fucker is costing us everything."

Darren looked pained. "I can try to get you a job in a lab or… I mean… the point is to blend in so they don't find you."

"Fuck," I said again. My eyes began to sting, and I turned away from him.

Jacey tugged on my arm. "Let's go for a swim."

She was right. I needed to cool off. "Swimsuits?" I managed, my voice gruff.

"No. They'll just get in the way," she whispered in my ear.

And a fuck. Today wasn't all bad, then.

I slid my hand into Jacey's, and we walked out the back door of the cabin toward the lake.

Once we got to the edge of the doc, Jacey shimmied out of her sundress, panties, and bra. She climbed down a convenient side ladder and into the lake.

I kicked off my pants and boxers and tore off my shirt, then went in after her.

The cold water hit me. "Holy shit!"

"It is a little cold," she admitted.

"A little? Fuck!" I walked across the sandy bottom to pull Jacey to me, absorbing her warmth.

"It won't feel as cold once you're inside me," she said.

I laughed, teeth chattering at the same time. "I think it might have shriveled up into my intestines by now.

She reached under the water and began working my cock with long, firm strokes.

I groaned and braced myself against one of the dock legs. "You sure know how to make a man feel better." I sighed, tilting her chin up and kissing her hungrily.

Jacey got me hard in no time. Then she climbed me, and I lined my dick up with her entrance.

She sank down on me, and we both moaned.

"I love you," I said, kissing her again as I moved her up and down on my cock. "I love you so much."

"I love you, too," she replied. "And maybe you can't be a doctor. But I can make you a daddy again."

Her words lit a fire of purpose in my gut, and I started fucking her harder and faster.

Jacey's tits bounced enticingly as I rammed her, her head thrown back, mouth open in silent ecstasy. "Yes, Daddy, fuck me hard. Fill me up with your baby juice."

I couldn't be a doctor. But this I could do. I angled her so I hit just the right spot with every one of my thrusts. "Are you gonna make me a daddy?" I asked as she cried out my name.

Her muscles clamped around me, milking me for my seed, and I poured into her with a cry of my own. I hiccuped a sob as I mumbled my hopes and dreams in her ear, some I could have, some that I couldn't.

"I'm gonna make you a daddy, Daddy," Jacey promised. She wrapped herself around me. "You get to have that."

I got hard all over again and turned with Jacey in my arms so her back was pressed against the post. "Baby…"

"Give it to me, Daddy. Give it to me hard." Her smile was pure temptation, and I groaned.

I nipped and sucked her lips then her neck as I pounded her against that post. I got so deep inside with the post for leverage that I swore I bottomed out.

Jacey whimpered, but encouraged me with her heels digging into my back. I trusted her to tell me if it was too much.

When I came, this time it was with her, both of us screaming our pleasure to the quiet lake.

A couple of loons were disturbed by our cries and took off, their wings slapping the water as they got themselves up and going.

We laughed. I waited a few minutes, then gently pulled out of Jacey, kissing her bruised skin and fondling her breasts.

"I suppose we should go back in before we freeze to death," she said, stroking my hair, getting it wet.

"I suppose we should," I agreed. We climbed up the ladder, then realized we hadn't brought towels. Laughing again, we sat on the edge of the dock, waiting to air dry.

Jacey leaned her head against my shoulder, and I absently rubbed one of her nipples as we watched nature around us. "I wonder if we could live here," she asked.

"It is nice," I said. "We'll have to ask Darren if this is a permanent or temporary thing."

"Yeah." We both fell silent, letting the water lap at our feet.

Speaking of laps, I pulled Jacey into mine, letting her lie back against my chest. I fondled her breasts and pinched her nipples, making her arch into me.

My cock slid inside her easily, and she chuckled. "I knew you had an ulterior motive."

"Sorry, baby, I just can't get enough," I replied.

She rocked in my lap, inching my dick in and out.

Our next orgasm was rather tame, but we came together, and I did manage to find more in my balls to give her to hopefully create a little life. I hugged my arms around her, splaying my hands over her belly.

We did dry eventually, and I helped Jacey stand and put her clothes on before pulling on mine. We walked hand-in-hand back to the house.

Darren was sitting in a chair in the living room, staring at something we couldn't see. He was frowning.

"Hey," I said as we walked in. "Long time no—" My words died on my lips.

Sitting across from Darren, holding guns, were two men in jackets that read 'FBI.'

"Um… we were just leaving," I wheezed and gave Jacey a shove toward the back door again.

"Caleb, Jacey, stay," a familiar voice said from the side of the room still hidden from my sight.

Fuuuuuuuuuuuuuuuuuck. "Jacey, go," I said, knowing she was not in the gunmen's sights but I was.

They cocked their weapons, and Masterson stood, walking to the middle of the room. "Jacey, stay."

I knew she wouldn't leave, but I had to beg anyway. "Don't worry about me, go!"

She shook her head and padded obediently to my side, clutching my arm.

"There she is." Masterson smiled at us. "It has been quite the wild ride trying to find you, and expensive to boot, but, as you must know by now, I always win."

"I thought we had a guard detail," I hissed to Darren, even though it was useless now.

"Oh you did. They're dead," Masterson replied for him cheerfully.

Darren didn't move or speak.

I started to get a bad feeling. "Darren?"

"Come closer, Caleb. You might as well see the consequences of your actions," Masterson said.

I stepped forward, and so did Jacey. When I saw the bloody hole in Darren's chest, however, I quickly buried her face in my shoulder, not letting her see.

"The man just did not know when to stay down," Masterson tsked.

"Shit, man, do you have to kill *everyone* we know?!" I asked.

"If you keep running away, apparently, I do," Masterson said.

"He's dead?" Jacey's voice was muffled against my shirt.

I swallowed. "Yeah. Yeah, he is."

She let out a soft sob.

"If it makes you feel any better, I didn't punish your parents or poor little Timothy for your actions," Masterson said. His eyes narrowed. "But if you ever do this again, that will not be the case."

"Fuck you, Masterson," I seethed.

He just laughed. "I like your spirit, Caleb. Crushing it is going to be one of the most satisfying things I've ever done."

Jacey shook in my arms, and I hugged her tighter. "So I guess it's back to the manor with us, huh? Can't be trusted with an apartment?"

"That fire took out the whole floor, and the floors above and below. It was a miracle no one was killed," Masterson said. "But, yes, not only is the apartment unavailable, you've shown you can't be trusted to stay there."

"God, this isn't happening," Jacey whispered.

"I'm not bringing you back to the estate, however. I need you in Minneapolis so you can be at work, doing my bidding, and on time," Masterson continued. "So, I have no choice but to put you in The Bunker."

That sounded ominous. "'The Bunker'?" I repeated.

"It's an underground safe house beneath the Masterson building. No one is getting you out of there," Masterson snickered. "Not even with dynamite."

My throat went dry. "That doesn't sound like a place we want to go."

"Tough." Masterson's voice lost all its good humor. "I'm tired of how much cost you two rack up. It's exhausting. I'm going to keep you right under me where I can see you. All. The. Time."

"I thought that was the idea behind the apartment," I said. "There were cameras everywhere."

"Yes. But that wasn't enough, now was it?" Masterson gestured to his two goons. "Get them in the car. I want to get out of this podunk place as soon as possible."

I stepped backward far enough that Jacey couldn't see the blood and gore that was Darren's chest. Then I carefully turned her and put my arm around her.

The goons flanked us and muscled us out the front door to a large, black Escalade.

"We're going to be okay," I told Jacey as they opened the door.

"No we're not," Jacey whispered.

BOOM!

-Jacey-

I rested my head on Caleb's shoulder as we drove away from the cabin. Masterson sat in the front seat with the driver, one of his goons. We were in the back with the other goon.

"How stupid did you have to be to think you could escape me?" Masterson chortled.

"Pretty stupid," Caleb replied flatly.

"Indeed. And you didn't even jump states! Fools," Masterson went on, still laughing to himself.

The goon sitting just in front of us in the Escalade turned and grinned at us, enjoying Masterson's little victory party. He also gave me the slow once-over, which I did not appreciate.

Caleb punched him in the nose. "Eyes ahead, buddy."

As his nose gushed blood, the goon reached for his gun, but Masterson stopped him with a delicate clearing of his throat. "Hunter, that's really not appropriate. And if you want to keep your eyes where they are, I'd suggest you keep them off my property."

Hunter grunted, but put his gun away.

"And Caleb, you really do need to work on that temper of yours," Masterson said, but grinned while he was saying it.

"I don't have a temper," Caleb seethed. "Except when it comes to Jacey. And you."

"And your stepfather, I would assume," Masterson replied.

Caleb ground his teeth. "And Hank."

"I'm honored to have made it above him on your list," Masterson chuckled. "It gives me a warm, gooey feeling inside."

"There's nothing warm and gooey inside you," Caleb said.

Masterson inclined his head. "Fair point."

Hunter watched us in the rearview mirror, now that Masterson had told him to face front. Masterson himself didn't bother to hide his regard, but because he was two seats ahead of us, Caleb couldn't do anything to him.

Which, I assumed, was the point.

"You sure know how to pick them, Caleb," he drawled, staring at me in a way that made me very uncomfortable. "Just when I think she's just your glorified fuck-toy, she jumps out a broken window in the middle of a fire and rappels down the side of a building. Courageous little thing."

"She's not going to be one of your interns, Masterson, so whatever sick thoughts you're having right now, you can just forget them," Caleb said.

"Oh, I'm going to fuck her eventually. And I'm going to make you watch," he smirked.

"Fat chance." Caleb scowled at Masterson.

My throat had closed with fear, and I dug my nails into Caleb's thigh when Masterson pulled out a gun and aimed it right at us.

"Maybe we should find an obliging rest stop and get it over with," he said. "In fact, let's."

The driver nodded, and we veered off the highway at the next blue sign.

As soon as the Escalade rolled to a stop, Caleb unbuckled and launched himself at Masterson.

Hunter, however, was faster and gripped Caleb by the throat. "Whoa there, Mr. Death-Wish. The boss wants you to watch him fuck your girl. You're going to watch him fuck your girl."

"We'll take turns," Masterson added evilly. "You can have my sloppy seconds."

I made a little "eep" sound in my throat, but I could also see Hunter squeezing Caleb's neck tighter and tighter. "Okay," I whispered. "I'll do it. Just leave him alone."

"Granted," Masterson replied as though I'd made a wish to a genie. "Get in the back. Hunter, put the seats down."

Caleb struggled harder when I climbed over the back seat and waited for Masterson to come to me. He circled the Escalade and opened the back hatch, crawling inside.

While Hunter held Caleb, the driver came to a side door and lowered the back seat, giving Masterson and me more room.

"Now, let me see those luscious breasts of yours," Masterson said.

My eyes welling with tears, I took off my shirt and bra.

He stared lasciviously at my breasts. "So nice. Caleb, you've been keeping her all to yourself all this time? Selfish of you."

Tears rolled down my cheeks as Masterson opened his pants.

Caleb kicked out, trying to hit Masterson, but failing. He gurgled when Hunter squeezed even harder.

I watched as Masterson slowly stroked himself. He was drawing this out, enjoying Caleb's and my pain.

"Touch it," Masterson ordered me, offering me his cock.

My hand shook as I reached out.

The car rocked with a sudden explosion, flames shooting up next to the passenger side of the Escalade.

Masterson fell back and smacked his head on the window hard enough to draw blood. He groaned.

Another explosion had Hunter letting go of Caleb and reaching for his gun. Caleb scrambled over to me and threw himself over me, protecting me with his body, and the Escalade kept rocking with explosions outside.

There was a tiny pinging sound, and then Hunter was dead, draped over the seat with a bullet hole in his head.

Then the back hatch was wrenched open, and a man in black with a ski mask on beckoned to Caleb and me. "Let's get the *fuck* out of here!"

We had no idea who our rescuer was, but anything beat fucking Masterson, so Caleb yanked me out of the Escalade, and we ran after the man in black.

A black Jeep skidded to a stop in front of us, and the man in black shoved us into the back, another man dressed just like him behind the wheel.

Caleb pulled off his shirt and jammed it onto me as the Jeep skidded away from the burning scene.

"Think Masterson will die?" he asked our rescuers. "Is the Escalade going to blow up?"

"I certainly hope not," the man who'd saved us said.

"Why? Because you're the good guys?" I asked, remembering what Darren had once said.

He snorted. "No. Because it will be harder to ransom you to him if he dies."

Caleb paled, and I gripped his arm.

"Don't look so surprised," the man who rescued us laughed. "And don't be scared. We don't want to get any scratches on the merchandise. Besides, maybe the Feds will pay more."

"We're going to be in some sort of bidding war?" Caleb asked.

He nodded. "Online auction. There are a lot of parties interested in you, and we thought we might as well take advantage."

"Who exactly?" Caleb responded, frowning.

"Eh, FBI, CIA, the alphabet agencies, you know. Masterson. Masterson's enemies. Masterson's friends," he ticked them off on his fingers. "Let's just say you two are hot commodities."

"And when is this auction?" Caleb asked.

"In a week," he replied. "Gotta get it all set up and get the word out, you know."

Caleb put an arm around me. "What hellhole are we staying in?"

"Just a room with live camera feed. Have to be able to showcase the merchandise," the man said. "You'll have food, water, and access to a bathroom. Mattress on the floor. It's not the Hilton, but you won't die."

"Comforting," Caleb muttered.

He turned back to look at us. "Now, I know you two are famous for causing trouble. I'd suggest you don't. My friend here is a crack shot, and let me tell you right now, if we don't get to sell you, nobody does, if you catch my meaning."

My mouth went dry. There was nothing in those dead eyes. No mercy. No remorse. Nothing.

"Understood," Caleb said.

"Good." He faced the front again.

The Jeep descended into silence. I gripped Caleb's hand for dear life as we went down the highway, then off-roading into the woods.

We were bounced all around but finally ended up at a carport that was covered with camouflage fabric. Our captors escorted us out of the Jeep with little fanfare. Caleb and I both wanted to live, after all, and I'd seen how accurate these two could be with a gun.

The two men brought us to a hatch about a mile away that was covered in more camouflage fabric. The driver opened it and gestured for us to go down without speaking a word. Come to think of it, he hadn't said one thing since we'd been captured.

Motion-sensing LED lights went on once we got into the bunker. I looked up to see if our captors would follow us but blinked in surprise as one of them waved to us, then closed the hatch.

Caleb and I were alone.

We listened to the hatch lock into place, then nothing, not even their footsteps.

It occurred to me that the bunker was probably soundproofed.

"Soundproofed," Caleb grunted my thought aloud.

I nodded.

"Well, it's not going to work, but might as well try," he sighed and climbed the ladder to the hatch. He wrenched at the handle, putting his bare shoulder against the hatch, but it didn't so much as twitch.

He descended the ladder and hugged me. "I hope the FBI has deep pockets," he murmured.

Despair choked me, and I buried my face in Caleb's naked shoulder. "Masterson will buy us. Or some other very bad organization. And if the FBI does manage to buy us back, then what? Darren's gone. He thought he'd gotten us to safety, but he was wrong. This just keeps happening to us."

Caleb rubbed my back. "We can't give up, Jacey." He nestled his chin in my hair.

"I don't want to give up, but I don't know how this ends," I all but wailed. I was afraid I was about to give into hysterics and gripped his waist.

"It ends with us going to school and having beautiful little babies who look just like you," he said, but I doubted his confidence. Caleb kissed my hair. "Regardless, we're together."

I nodded. That much was true. "I hope they're selling us as a package deal. I don't want us to be apart in all this."

He grimaced. "I hope so, too."

I pulled away from him and stripped off my shirt, eyeing the tiny shower in the corner of the bunker.

"What's wrong?" Caleb asked me.

"I need to wash him off me." I shuddered. "I need his touch to go away."

He nodded and helped me out of my pants and panties. Then he took off his own.

"Is there room enough in there for both of us?" I asked, looking doubtfully at the shower.

"We'll make it work." He kissed me and backed me to the shower.

I was glad for his body heat because when we turned on the shower, it was cold. No amount of adjusting would make it warm up, either.

My teeth chatter, but I put Caleb's hand on the breast Masterson had touched. "Make him go away," I begged.

Caleb did more than that. He pushed me back against the shower wall, his shoulders almost too wide for the space. I felt his cock push into me as he rubbed my breasts possessively.

"Yes, Caleb, yes," I moaned, widening my legs as far as they would go in the tiny space. "Take me."

"I fucking am," he growled, bouncing me up so my legs were wrapped around his waist. "I am fucking taking what's mine."

I laugh breathlessly. "Marking your territory?"

"That's right," Caleb grunted. He had me hard and fast but still managed to force two orgasms out of my body before he came himself.

We panted, leaning against the shower wall and each other.

Then Caleb pulled out gently and cupped my sex with his hand. "Who does this belong to?"

"You," I said without hesitation.

"That's right." He then grabbed his cock. "Who does this belong to?"

"Me," I smile tiredly.

"Good. Now that's settled. Should we try to find something to eat before I take you over there on that mattress?" he asked.

I blushed. "In front of all those people who want to buy us?"

"Hell yes. I want them to know that they *will* keep their grubby hands off you," Caleb decided.

I stroked his cheek. "Yes."

"Is that a 'yes' to food or a 'yes' to me claiming every part of your body?" he asked.

"Both. Any. All." I looped my arms around his neck and kissed him. "I love you."

Caleb smiled and kissed me back. "I love you, too."

SOLD!

-Caleb-

I sat cross-legged on the bed with Jacey sitting across from me while we ate rehydrated pot roast from ration packs. We balanced the food on our knees while our bottled waters rested on the floor next to us.

We'd been picnicking this way for days. We'd also been doing it missionary style so I could hide most of Jacey from the camera. Or cameras. I wasn't quite sure how many cameras were on us.

They'd left us clothes as well, so Jacey and I spent most of our time in wind-suits. When we weren't fucking. We spent a lot of time fucking. Mostly because we were bored.

There was no television. No phone. No computer. Nothing but Jacey, me, food, clothing, water, and a mattress. And the corner of our bunker that was a small bathroom. That shower had gotten a lot of miles, too.

"I'm two weeks past when I should have gotten my period," she told me while I was munching on my pot roast.

I choked, grabbed water, gulped, then beat my chest and coughed. "Jacey, give a man a little warning!"

She bit her lip. "I'm worried about having a baby now."

"Me, too," I admitted, putting my hand on her knee. "I thought we were safe before. Now, I don't know. But I'm going to take care of you and a little one if we are blessed to have one."

"Will it really be a blessing right now?" Jacey asked softly. Her eyes were filled with worry.

"It will always be a blessing, no matter what the circumstances. It'll be hard right now, but it would still be a blessing," I assured her.

"Okay." She put her hand over mine and squeezed gently.

Crackling filled the air, or cackling, or both. I snapped my head up to see a loudspeaker in one corner of the room.

"You missed your period because you've got an IUD implant." I recognized the voice of one of our captors. "Masterson had it put in right after you gave birth to Will Jr."

Jacey paled and set my food aside so I could stand and face the speaker. "The hell? How do you know that, and how is it any of your business?"

"Masterson told us we weren't going to get a third hostage," he said. "We're still negotiating price, but suffice to say, I think you're going home to daddy."

"I don't suppose, if we asked nicely, you'd just let us go?" I tried.

He laughed. "You're funny. I'm gonna miss you."

"Wish I could say the feeling was mutual," I grunted back.

"Why don't you two just occupy yourselves with more fucking. That's always fun to watch," he said.

"Cute." I took my rations to the trash and dumped them. Suddenly, I wasn't hungry anymore.

"Oh, wait, wait, we've got a bidder coming up from behind. Looks like the CIA wants you pretty badly," he informed us.

I perked up. "Really? The CIA? That's great. Sell us to them."

"They're really only interested in one of you," he tsked.

I scowled. "You can go ahead and tell them they're not getting shit out of either of us if we're separated. We're a package deal."

"Noted." I could hear furious typing on the other end of the line.

"I think it's a live auction," Jacey whispered to me.

"I think so, too." I sat down next to her on the bed. "You finished with that?"

She nodded, and I took her food to the trash as well. Then I just sat with my arm around her as we got the blow-by-blow on our precarious future from the speaker in the corner of the ceiling.

"Oh look, the FBI doesn't want the CIA to have you. Bidding is going up and up," our captor chuckled.

"I don't suppose you could just sell us to one of them and take your money and be happy, could you?" I suggested.

"Nah. They're going to beat the sheik, anyway," he said.

"Sheik?" Jacey mouthed to me.

"Masterson has enemies. The sheik is one of them. Oh, wait, we've got… yes, I think they might even outdo the sheik!" he crowed.

"The CIA?" I asked hopefully.

"The FBI?" Jacey said.

He snorted. "You two are far too hopeful for your own good. No, not the CIA or the FBI. As far as I can tell, they're out of the running."

"Shit," I muttered.

Jacey crawled into my lap, and I held her to me. If we weren't going to be bought by an alphabet agency, then any other buyer was just going to be a new kind of hell, and we knew it.

"This is a lot more fun than I thought," our captor chuckled. "Just seeing bids go up and up. I might be able to afford that private island when we're done here."

"How nice for you," I sneered.

"All right, six billion going once, six billion going twice…" he murmured.

Six billion? That certainly wasn't an alphabet agency.

"Sold! Six billion dollars for Caleb," he said.

"Just for Caleb?" Jacey gaped.

"Just for Caleb. Bidding's still open on you. I think you might only top out at three billion, but we'll see if we can't get four," he mused.

Jacey clung to me, and I wrapped my arms more tightly around her. "We're a package deal," I said again.

"Not necessarily. Come on lucky number four billion." He began clapping excitedly.

Except for the clapping, our captor was finally, blessedly silent. Then he let out a shout and I could almost see him doing a fist pump in the air. "Four billion! Yes!"

I put a hand at the back of Jacey's neck and stroked her skin. My heart was pounding, and her breath was coming in frightened little pants. "Same person?" I asked cautiously.

"Pfft. You're so cute when you're hopeful. Of course not," he said.

"I told you we're a package deal. So you'll just have to accept an offer that includes both of us," I insisted.

"Oh yeah? And what do you think you're gonna do about it?" he scoffed.

I didn't have an answer for that one.

"And, just in case you were planning to do something stupid..." Clouds of gas began to descend from what I thought were sprinkler heads in the ceiling.

"Fuck!" I coughed, pulling Jacey onto the floor with me. But it was no use. In less than two minutes, we were out.

I woke up tied to a chair wearing only boxer shorts. I had no idea where I was, but the floor was marble, the walls were tile, and Jacey wasn't there. The only one of those that concerned me was that Jacey wasn't there.

"Ah. He wakes." A man in a long robe paced before me. "Do you know who I am?"

"I'm guessing the sheik?" I replied, looking him over. "Where's Jacey?"

"She is with the Trinary. You were quite expensive on your own. I did not feel she had the same value you do," he said.

I struggled against the ropes binding me, but they were so tight they cut into my wrists and ankles. "She's valuable to me."

"Yes, a woman always is," he responded dismissively.

"I'm not telling you shit unless I get Jacey," I declared.

He chuckled. "Of course you are. You want to be able to stand again when I'm finished with you, I'm sure. And have children."

I heard a sizzle behind me and jumped, cranking my head around.

There was a brazier of burning coal behind me and a man holding an iron brand. My mouth went dry.

"Fuck," I whispered.

"Now, then. I want to know everything you know about Masterson's operations in Brazil," the sheik said. "For a start."

"I want Jacey," I replied.

He shook his head. "You are a fool."

The man with the hot poker approached me.

"Maybe you need a taste in order to understand just how serious I am," the sheik said.

I swallowed. The poker hovered scant inches from my upper thigh, and I could feel the heat. "Will you at least TRY to get Jacey?"

"I'll consider it, depending on the information you give me," the sheik responded.

There was a difference between being courageous and being an idiot, and I had a feeling the sheik was about to educate me in that difference unless I got my shit together. I couldn't very well go save Jacey if I couldn't walk.

"A question for a question," I bargained.

The sheik raised an eyebrow, then a smile played at the corners of his lips. "Ibrahim, we won't be needing the poker right now."

Ibrahim looked disappointed, but thankfully, the poker moved away from my genitals and back to the brazier.

"What is Masterson doing in Brazil?" the sheik asked again.

"He just massacred a village of endangered indigenous people to continue his illegal logging operations there," I said without hesitation.

"Where?" he demanded.

I shook my head. "My turn for a question."

He laughed. "So it is."

"What is the Trinary?" I asked.

"A group of three very dangerous assassins who pool their resources on occasion and help each other out from time to time," he replied. "Now, where?"

I gave him latitude and longitude coordinates. Those coordinates would be burned into my brain forever because I knew I'd arranged a slaughter there.

"Excellent. Ibrahim, are you taking notes?" he asked.

Ibrahim came back into view holding an electronic tablet. He was making quick notes on it with his fingertips.

"Where is the Trinary?" I continued my line of questioning.

"What? You think you're going to go find them?" He threw back his head and guffawed loudly. "Caleb Killeen, you have some balls, I'll give you that. The Trinary does not operate out of any one location. You would have to seek them out on the dark web."

"Then I will," I said.

He wiped moisture from the corner of his eye. "I very much doubt you will have the opportunity, but we'll see, won't we? Now, about Canada..."

"It's run by a man named Girard, if that helps. He has several locations there. I was only at two, and I have no idea where they are except somewhere near Uppsala because we were basically dragged through the wilderness to get there," I responded.

"Ah, yes, well, I don't suppose you can know *everything* he's doing, but that doesn't count as an answer. I still have my question," he said.

"Shoot," I replied.

"Masterson has been interfering with my human trafficking operations. My shipments have been diverted more than once, and he has taken my profit. I am... displeased about this," he continued. "What do you know about the human trafficking operation?"

"He had to destroy a shipment not long ago," I said. I gave the sheik dates and locations of the next shipments coming in. "He also has a thriving underage sex ring going on throughout the United States and Canada."

He grimaced. "That was my shipment he destroyed. I was trying to divert it back, and the bastard decided if he couldn't have them, he was going to break my toys. I was… displeased."

I was getting the impression it was not a good idea to "displease" the sheik. "Well, hopefully, as long as he doesn't change the locations, you'll be able to get some of your own back. Is the Trinary going to treat Jacey well?"

"I have no idea what the Trinary intends to do with Jacey. She certainly has less knowledge than you do," he said.

"That's not true," I corrected him. "I told Jacey everything. Everything I knew."

His eyebrows went up. "Then they got the same information at a much lower price. Pity."

"If it makes you feel any better, I don't think Jacey knows the coordinates in Brazil," I replied.

"It does indeed." He stroked his chin. "Now, Caleb. About his dealings in illegal antiquities…"

The questions went on for hours, long after I'd run out of questions of my own. The sun went down, and the moon rose outside the windows before the sheik called it a night.

"We will talk more tomorrow," he warned me. "Ibrahim, take him to his room."

"Can I have limited access to a computer?" I requested as Ibrahim undid my wrists and ankles. I'd long ago pissed myself because the sheik wouldn't let me use the bathroom, and my feet were nearly blue and had lost feeling. Ibrahim had to help me stand.

"We will talk more tomorrow," he repeated.

Then he was gone, and it was Ibrahim and me.

THE TRINARY

-Jacey-

I woke up in the dark. The first thing I noticed was that Caleb wasn't there. I felt around for him, but the space I was in was tiny, only big enough for me to lie down, curled up on the floor. So, I knew almost immediately that I was alone. Without Caleb.

Panicking, I felt along the walls for a way out. I found a door handle, but jiggling it did not cause it to yield.

I banged on the metal door and screamed for help.

The door swung open, and three black-clad figures stood before me, their faces covered by half-masks over their noses and mouths.

"She's awake," one of them told the others.

"Thank you, Captain Obvious," another, this one a female judging by her voice, said.

Captain Obvious muttered something about her being a raging bitch, but the third person grabbed my arms and dragged me out of the tiny space.

"You were an expensive little thing," he chuckled, standing me up and marching me to a metal chair in a small, empty, concrete space.

"Sorry?" I replied, though I wasn't sure what I was apologizing for. I didn't run the auction, after all.

"You will be if you don't talk," Captain Obvious said, putting a small knife to my throat.

I was afraid to swallow. I was afraid to even breathe, thinking I might cut myself on his blade.

"Lay off her. We haven't even asked any questions yet." Chuckles sighed, smacking the blade out of Captain Obvious's hand. It went skidding across the room.

When Captain Obvious went to retrieve it, Chuckles knelt in front of me. "We know you miss your boyfriend, but he was too rich for our blood. You almost were, too."

"Four billion dollars is a lot different than six, I suppose," I muttered.

"Exactly." Chuckles smoothed his hands over my thighs, parting them.

I tried to scootch away, but either the chair was bolted to the floor or it was too heavy to scrape across the concrete.

He grinned at me. "Only the boyfriend gets this privilege, huh?"

"Yes," I responded firmly.

"That's sweet." Raging Bitch circled me like a prowling panther. "I think we can leave her alone for the time being. She hasn't refused to answer our questions yet."

"We haven't asked her any," Captain Obvious pointed out.

She raised an eyebrow at him in annoyance. "Yes. We know."

"Where's Caleb?" I demanded. "I'm not answering any questions until I get to see Caleb!"

The three looked at each other then burst out laughing.

"Oh, darling, it's so adorable that you think you're in charge here." Raging Bitch snickered. She put one pointy, perfectly-manicured nail under my chin. "Unfortunately, for you, you're not."

I swallowed then winced as she flicked her nail over my skin, drawing blood.

"Oh sure, Catwoman here can draw all the blood she wants, but I take out one teensy little knife…" Captain Obvious complained.

"Last time we questioned someone, you slit their throat before we got any useful information." Chuckles grunted.

"He insulted my mother!" Captain Obvious argued.

The other two just shook their heads.

"I want to know where Caleb is," I insisted again. I wasn't going to let them bully me into being silent. Without Caleb, it didn't really matter what they did to me, anyway.

"He's with the sheik. There, happy now?" Captain Obvious said. "He's an entire continent away from you."

Shit. "What happens after I answer your questions?" I asked cautiously.

"You can go on your merry way just as soon as we're sure we have all the information we can get out of you," Raging Bitch replied.

I nodded. "All right. What do you want to know?"

THEY GRILLED me for hours about everything Caleb had told me. I answered to the best of my ability, but I didn't know specific locations or anything like that.

Captain Obvious wanted to cut off my fingers at the end to make sure I was really telling the truth, but Raging Bitch and Chuckles stopped him. He pouted, twirling his knife between his fingers.

"And that's all you know?" Raging Bitch asked once my mouth was dry and my tongue felt like leather in my mouth.

"Yeth," I responded, trying to moisten my mouth. "Wather?"

"Get her some water," Chuckles said to Captain Obvious.

"Why do I have to do it?" he whined.

"Because I told you to," Chuckles growled.

He sighed and got a bottle of water out of a nearby black duffel bag. He handed it to me with a scowl. "Drink up."

I twisted the cap and it cracked, so I assumed the water hadn't been tampered with.

It turned out I was wrong.

I gagged on the water, coughing and retching. Raging Bitch grabbed my chin and forced the water down my throat. It tasted bitter.

The three waited a few minutes, Raging Bitch's hand over my mouth so I couldn't throw up. Then Chuckles started to ask questions again.

"Who are you working with?" he asked.

"Caleb," I replied automatically, my stomach roiling from whatever they'd given me.

"And who's he working with?" Chuckles continued.

"Masterson." I urped a little, but Captain Obvious put the knife under my chin, almost daring me to try to throw up. "But we don't want to. We were with the FBI, but Masterson hit our safe house..."

I just kept talking and talking, babbling, and answering all of their questions.

"So, you're Will Jr.'s mother, huh?" Raging Bitch asked, sounding excited.

I snorted. "Yeah, but Masterson doesn't care about that. He wants to mess with Caleb."

"And the easiest way to do that is to dangle you over his head," Chuckles mused. "Sicko bastard."

"He wants to fuck me," I slurred, blinking as the world became blurry. "He wanted me to touch his dick in the Escalade, but the auctioneers got us out first."

"Good to know he hasn't changed that much over the years," Raging Bitch muttered.

"What do you guys want with Masterson, anyway?" I asked.

The three laughed again. "Let's just say he owes us for services rendered and needs to pay up."

"Okay. So... now that I don't know anything else, can I go?" I said.

"Why would we give up Masterson's favorite toy?" Chuckles grinned.

Oh no. "But you said I could go," I argued.

"Yeah, about that. We lied." Raging Bitch winked at me.

I kicked out at Chuckles, and he yelped when I hit his shin. "I want Caleb!"

"Princess, you can't have him. You're probably not going to see him again in this lifetime." Chuckles seethed. "Especially if you keep kicking me."

With an angry harrumph, I stopped kicking and folded my arms. "What, now are you going to try to get your money back by ransoming me to Masterson?"

"No, we don't want him to have his toys back," Raging Bitch said. "But we might ransom you to the sheik."

"Good," I replied, feeling hopeful. "Then Caleb and I can be together."

"You probably have that sweet little idea that as long as you're together, everything's going to be okay." Chuckles snorted.

Captain Obvious made a gagging noise.

"Trust me. You're toast. Both of you. No matter where you are. No matter where you go. Whether you're together or apart. Right now, you're both just pawns in the game," Raging Bitch said.

I squared my shoulders. "I don't believe that. We're going to get out of this."

"That, at least, will be fun to watch." Captain Obvious snickered.

Then the two men grabbed me and dragged me back to the tiny hole in the wall they'd put me in before.

"Hey! What about food? Real water?" I asked. "Bathroom break, for the love of God!"

"Sorry, Princess. This isn't a hotel." They tossed me in. "See you around."

"Hey!" I cried again, but the door slammed shut. I beat on it with my fists, but a heavy bolt slid into place.

I screamed for an hour, but nobody came. I couldn't hear a thing outside my tiny room. Maybe it was soundproofed? I didn't know. I just knew I'd torn my fingernails to the nub trying to find a way out. Something to grab. Something to move. Something to break. But there was nothing.

Holding back a sob, I curled into a ball on the floor. The room was freezing, I realized now.

I didn't know how long I shivered in the dark. It could have been hours. It could have been days. But finally, the door opened again.

Captain Obvious leaned in the doorway. "Looks like you need some cleaning up."

Shaking, I got to my knees.

"I like the change in attitude." Captain Obvious led me out into the main room again.

This time, in the middle, was a camp shower with a privacy screen. Raging Bitch was holding a green sundress.

"Hop in and clean up. We've got a plane to catch," she told me.

I stepped behind the privacy screen, knowing Chuckles and Captain Obvious were on the other side, and took the fastest shower I'd ever taken in my life. After drying off with a towel that felt like sandpaper, I pulled on the dress, distressed it was sans bra or underwear, but at least they gave me sandals to wear.

Once I was finished, Raging Bitch grabbed me by the arm and dragged me toward a different door in the room.

Chuckles whistled. "You fill out that dress real nice."

"Save it. We said no sampling the merchandise. Remember? That was the agreement," Raging Bitch said.

Captain Obvious and Chuckles looked disappointed but kept their hands off me nonetheless. In the SUV. In the jet. All the way through the cobblestone streets of a country I didn't recognize.

It took a whole day, but finally we stopped outside a villa on a high hill outside of a town. The wrought iron gates opened, and we drove inside.

When the black sedan came to a stop, Raging Bitch reached over me and opened the car door. She shoved me out so I fell to my knees on the stairs outside the front door, scraping them and my palms.

"Enjoy your new home," she called sweetly. Then the door slammed closed, and the three of them took off.

I struggled to my feet, standing alone inside a wide courtyard at the stairs to the main door of the villa. I hugged myself, wondering where I'd ended up this time.

The door suddenly opened, and a tall man with dark skin came walking out.

"Jacey?" he intoned.

I brushed gravel and a little bit of blood off my knees. "Yes, sir."

"Follow me." The man turned back into the villa.

My stomach knotted, but I followed him, climbing the stairs and going through the heavy wooden door into a hacienda-style villa.

"D-Do you mind if I ask where we are?" I asked as I followed the man.

"Spain." He grunted, but said nothing more.

"You have a nice house," I continued, hoping to maybe sweeten him up a little.

"It's not mine," he grunted back.

"Oh." I fell silent, walking along a covered walkway to a large room where a man in long robes was holding court.

"Thank you, Ibrahim. That will be all," the new man said.

GOOD LITTLE BOYS AND GIRLS

-Caleb-

I was just coming out of the shower, a towel around my waist, when I saw someone on my bed.

The long, dark hair spread over my pillows reminded me so much of Jacey, it made my chest hurt. But I knew it couldn't be her.

It was another Spanish 'snack' the sheik meant to tempt me with for being a 'good boy.'

I sighed and braced one knee on the mattress so I could lean over and give the woman's shoulder a shake. "Come on, you. Get up and get out. Make sure the sheik pays you well for your time, but I'm really not interested."

The woman rolled on her back, and I felt like I'd been punched in the gut. It was Jacey!

"Caleb?" she sniffled.

"Oh, baby." I climbed fully onto the bed and pulled her into my lap, wrapping my arms around her. "Are you okay? Did they hurt you? How did you get here? Are you hurt?"

Jacey wrapped herself around me tightly, and I noted, as the skirt of her green sundress rode up, she wasn't wearing any underwear. "No. They just scared me a little, that's all."

"Why aren't you wearing underwear?" I asked, frowning. My dick, thickening under the towel, certainly didn't mind, but the rest of me was very concerned she'd been going around with a dress that only went to her knees without any underwear on.

"They didn't give me any." She buried her face in my neck. "I thought they'd sold me somewhere else, and I was never going to see you again."

"I was going to find you, no matter what." I pulled my towel off so my hard cock rested right at her entrance. "Jacey, I…"

She kissed me. "I need it, too." Then her beautiful body was taking me in.

I groaned and pushed my hand up under her dress to wrap my arm around her bare waist. "Anything else they didn't give you?" I asked, gently rocking my hips so I inched in and out of her.

In response, she reached down and pulled the sundress over her head, letting it fall to the other side of the bed.

"Oh, baby." I palmed her breast, bringing it to my lips to suck a nipple as we made slow love.

When Jacey made a sound in her throat that told me she needed more, I laid her back on the bed, one leg braced against my shoulder so she was wide open for me, and began thrusting in earnest.

Her nails dug into my arms.

"You want daddy to fill you with his hot cum?" I breathed in her ear, my balls smacking against her as I took her hard and fast.

"Yes, daddy. Fill me up," she moaned.

I rubbed her throbbing clit with my thumb and my beautiful Jacey came apart with the sweetest of cries. Then I groaned and gave her exactly what she wanted, shoving myself as deep as I could before pulsing my cum into her.

It probably wasn't the most romantic of 'baby, I've missed yous,' but it was what we needed.

When I moved to pull out, Jacey wrapped her legs around my waist and held me in place. "Where do you think you're going?" she asked.

I grinned and kissed her slowly, easing my tongue in and out of her mouth in a way that told her exactly what I planned to do to her body. "I was going to get us a drink of water, but if you don't need any…"

She wrapped her arms around me, too, kissing my neck and rubbing her breasts against my chest. "I just need you."

Truth be told, I was pretty needy, too. I cupped her ass and drew her hips against mine, forcing more of my still-hard cock into her body.

Jacey moaned, and her fingers spiked into my hair.

"Damn," I groaned as I felt her working my shaft with her inner muscles. "Baby, you don't have to try so hard. I'm already there." I pinched her nipple, and she gasped. "Nobody hurt you? You're sure?"

"They grabbed me kind of hard and threatened me with a knife, but no, I'm fine," she babbled as I started pounding her again. "I'm better than fine. I'm with you."

I saw the finger bruises on her arms, then, and the anger that bubbled up within me made me fuck her a little harder than I intended.

Luckily, Jacey was into it. Her nails dug into my scalp, her fingers twisted in my hair.

"Damn," I muttered and kissed her hard. "Baby, it's so hot you always take whatever I have to give you."

She smiled at me, and the world was all right again. I was inside the woman I loved, banging her just as hard as I wanted to, and she was smiling at me.

Now, if we were in a small suburban home with two-and-a-half kids and a dog, everything would be perfect.

Instead, we're inside some sultan's vacation home and completely at his mercy.

I was getting pretty tired of that.

Jacey put her hands on either side of my face. "Hey. Stay with me. It's okay. I'm here."

A tear slid down my cheek, and I turned my head to kiss her hand. "I'm sorry, baby. You're right. We gotta live in the moment."

I pressed my forehead to hers and concentrated only on the sex and being with her at last. I didn't want to admit it, but I'd been so scared I'd never see her again, that she was being hurt, that I couldn't help her, I hadn't slept in days.

Now she was here, and we were okay for the time being. That was something worth celebrating.

She arched underneath me, and I felt Jacey's whole body tremble as she came around my cock.

I wasn't proof against that. I came hard, filling her up, crushing my lips to hers as I pumped her full of everything that was left in my balls.

As the trembling subsided, we both clung tightly to each other. I stroked my thumbs over her hips, reassuring myself that she was still there. That she was real.

Jacey ran her hands up and down my back, probably confirming the same thing.

"I really think I should get you something to drink, love," I finally whispered in her ear. "You look beautiful, but also a mess. A beautiful mess."

She laughed and swatted me. "You're not supposed to tell the woman you're dating she looks like a mess."

"What, don't you remember, Mrs. Allan? We're married," I grinned. "And married people tell each other when they look wrecked."

"Well, someone with a *very* big dick just decided to wreck me," she sniffed. "I wonder who that could have been."

I let my eyes go wide and innocent. "No idea. Maybe I should check under the bed?"

Jacey laughed again. Then she cupped my cheek, rubbing her thumb under my eye. "Caleb, haven't you been sleeping?"

"Have you?" I countered.

She shook her head. "Not a wink. I was too scared."

I nuzzled her. "I didn't really care what happened to me. But I was scared for you. I… I tried holding out and not telling them anything until they brought you to me, but…"

"Same," she replied. "It's a lot harder than you think."

"They're just very good at threats." I very gently started to pull out of her again, but her legs locked around my waist and I sighed. "Jacey..."

"Just a little longer? Please? I'm not gonna die, I swear," she pleaded.

Shaking my head in consternation, I rolled on my back at least so I wasn't squashing her. "You are the most cock-possessive woman..."

"Don't finish that sentence. I don't want to know about any other woman you've ever been with," she warned me.

I swallowed the rest of my sentence. "Noted."

"But I'm glad to know I'm the most possessive." She smiled at me again, trailing her fingertips over my chest.

I caught her hand and kissed her fingers. "*Please* let me get you some water?"

"Are you getting some for yourself?" she asked.

"Cross my heart." I made the gesture over my pec. "Now please?"

With a sigh, she scooted backward, wriggling carefully off my dick. She curled up beside me on the bed.

I didn't wait for her to change her mind. I got up and went to the closet to the mini-fridge inside. I pulled out two bottles of water and came back to the bed.

Jacey reached for hers. Feigning innocence, I tapped it right against her nipple. She squeaked, and, like clockwork, her nipple hardened.

"Caleb!" she protested.

"Mhm?" I replied, ducking my head to suck on her peaked nipple.

"Ugh! You're incorrigible!" she giggled, giving up.

I let go of her nipple with one last lick then poked her water bottle. "Drink up."

She sat up next to me, and we both drank our water.

Jacey guzzled hers, and I was worried until I got distracted by the fact that some missed her mouth and dribbled down her chin and neck and over her chest.

"Is that an invitation?" I murmured, leaning in to lap it off her. The cool of the water and the warmth of her skin was a heady combination on my tongue.

There was a knock at the door, and I sat up. I grabbed her water and smacked it down next to mine on the bedside table, then yanked down the bedcovers and got Jacey situated so that she was covered up.

I slid off the bed and put on my boxers, padding to the door. "Yes?" I asked.

"The sheik would like you to join him for dinner," Ibrahim said on the other side of the door. "You and Miss Jacey. I have brought appropriate clothing for the occasion."

"Okay." I opened the door halfway, not wanting to expose Jacey, no matter how covered up she was.

Ibrahim smirked at me and handed me two sets of clothing. "I imagine you've been quite busy."

I bristled. "Yes, well, that's none of your business."

"I know. That's why I'm bothering you about it." He chuckled. "You are so easy to upset."

"Glad I can entertain you. Can I go now?" I asked.

Ibrahim craned his head, looking behind me. I turned and saw Jacey draw the covers up to her neck. "She is an exquisite creature. I cannot fault you on your taste."

"Gee, thanks. See you at dinner." I slammed the door in his face, likely hitting him in the nose.

The grunt of pain on the other side of the door told me I had.

"Why does everybody want to see me naked?" Jacey complained as I laid out our clothes on the end of the bed.

"Because you are, as Ibrahim said, 'exquisite,'" I replied, though I sounded more jealous than complimentary.

She dropped the covers and crawled off the bed, coming to stand behind me, looping her arms around my waist and kissing my shoulder. "I only want to see you naked. Does that make you feel any better?"

I pouted at her. "Some."

"What's got you so grumpy, still? He's gone," she said.

I pointed at the dress on the bed.

Jacey looked down and her eyes widened. "That's not a dress."

"Apparently, they think it is," I grumbled.

"I don't want to wear that! The V goes down to my belly button! And are those *two* slits up the sides?! They go all the way up to the waist!" Jacey complained.

I turned my head and kissed her, trying to tamp down on my own anger. "I don't want to make our host unhappy just yet. But I might try to work clothing choices into our conversation tonight."

"Caleb, I won't be able to wear a bra!" she screeched, turning the dress over and showing me it was backless.

"Okay, I'm not a fan of the dress either. But… I think we need to keep him happy for now," I said through my teeth.

"Well, all he gets to do is look," she muttered. Then she growled and held up what could not possibly be classified as underwear by the thong.

"I'll call Ibrahim," I grunted.

DINNER WITH THE SHEIK

-Jacey-

I resisted the urge to reach back and pull the thong out of my ass cheeks. It was only going to ride up again, and I didn't need to give Ibrahim or the sheik the satisfaction of seeing me uncomfortable.

Instead, I wore the ridiculous dress with my head held high. Caleb had tried to get Ibrahim to bring something else, but the man had just laughed at him. So, Caleb was now in a truly foul mood.

I wasn't sure if he knew whether walking in front of me or behind me was going to save the most of my modesty, but I also knew I had serious side-boob going on, and I had to resist the urge to tug at the fabric there as well.

"Next time he puts me in this getup, I demand you wear a Speedo," I grumbled.

"Next time he puts you in that getup, I'm going to punch him in the nose," Caleb grunted back.

We arrived in the gardens with Ibrahim still snickering to himself. The sheik was already seated at a wrought iron table. He smiled at us and gestured for us to sit.

Caleb went to pull out my chair, but Ibrahim beat him to it. I could practically hear the sizzle coming off Caleb as we both sat down.

"Caleb, Jacey, thank you for joining me. You both look very nice," the sheik grinned.

"Could we have a discussion about Jacey's wardrobe?" Caleb asked.

"No," the sheik replied. "I had a feeling you would have your objections, and, frankly, I don't care. If I don't get to touch, I at least want to look."

Caleb growled deep in his throat, and I placed a hand on his thigh. "It's just a bit… uncomfortable," I said to the sheik. "I don't usually run around half naked."

"I have videos we hacked from Masterson that beg to differ," the sheik chortled.

I felt a flush all over my skin and knew I must be beet red from head to toe. "I don't usually run around half naked when Caleb's not around."

"He's right here." The sheik gestured.

"Yes, but, I mean, you know, not with other people around," I stammered.

The sheik threw back his head and laughed. "I also have video from when you were being auctioned. Nice job blocking the camera, Caleb, but it's still obvious you were fucking."

"Isn't there anywhere we can go where people aren't watching us fuck?!" Caleb burst out.

The sheik laughed again. "Not when you make it look so pleasurable."

"There's a camera in our room," I sighed.

"There are several cameras in your room," he corrected me. "If Masterson can get his jollies watching you two, I don't see why I can't."

"It's not like we had a choice in the matter," Caleb seethed.

The sheik cocked his head. "Do you think you have a choice now?"

Caleb ground his teeth but ultimately hung his head in defeat. "No."

"There you go." Servants began coming in with decadent foods and laying them on the table. The sheik plucked a juicy black olive from one tray and popped it in his mouth. "See, this is another one of those situations where you don't have any choices. I could tell you to fuck Jacey right here on this table in front of me, and all you would be able to answer is, 'What positions, and how hard, sir?'"

"I'd… really rather not do that," I said softly.

"I know. That's why I'm not asking you to." He popped another olive in his mouth. "Caleb has been very helpful to my business, so I thought I'd give him a toy to play with, but he wasn't happy without you. It came at great expense to me, but I did get the opportunity to screw Masterson over several times, so you were worth it."

I blinked. "Uh… thanks?"

"You're welcome," the sheik replied. He patted his rotund belly. "I usually like to sample the finer things in life, and you would certainly be one of those. But it would make Caleb very difficult to deal with, so I've decided to leave it at getting a nice look every once in a while."

"That's… um… thanks?" I said again.

He chuckled. "Caleb's already pouting." He winked in Caleb's direction.

I looked over at Caleb and saw he was, indeed, glowering at the sheik.

"Caleb." I squeezed his knee. "Be nice."

"Oh, I like that," the sheik laughed. "A collar on the beast. Yes, you were worth every penny."

"Glad we can entertain you," Caleb muttered. But he did stop glaring.

"Young people in love are always entertaining. Especially young people as… active… as you two are." The sheik grinned and began working on a sprig of grapes. "Eat, eat. I don't want to be the only one eating."

I reached for some small pieces of cheese and began loading up my plate. Caleb took a few of the slivered ham slices and some oranges.

"You both have good taste." The sheik leaned forward as we

started to eat. "Now, just having you pisses Masterson off to no end, so that's a bonus, but I do want to see how useful I can make you from here on out."

Caleb stopped eating. "I don't know what you think we can do for you besides the information we gave you," he responded cautiously.

"Yes, that is the quandary." The sheik pulled thoughtfully on his beard. "I do have my own operations. You handled Masterson's so seamlessly, I thought I could use another assistant. For Ibrahim."

Ibrahim looked up from where he was standing against the wall. "Your Highness?"

"You work too hard, Ibrahim. Are you telling me you don't want an assistant?" the sheik asked.

Ibrahim looked over at me. "I think she has better assets."

Caleb hissed.

"Hmm. All right, an assistant for each of us, then. I'll take Caleb; you take Jacey," the sheik decided.

"How do I know he'll keep his hands to himself?" Caleb demanded.

The sheik raised an eyebrow. "Because I will tell him to. And when I tell Ibrahim to do something, he always does it. It's a quality I'd like to engender in you."

"I can do what I'm told. I just won't have Jacey constantly harassed," Caleb said.

"I won't promise she won't get harassed, but I will promise she won't be touched," the sheik replied.

Caleb's jaw worked. "Fine."

The sheik laughed. "It's so adorable that you think you have a choice."

"You said you didn't want me to pout all the time," Caleb pointed out.

"True, true." The sheik leaned back in his chair. "I can see why Masterson found you so entertaining. He likes to break his toys. I like to see them function properly. That way, you don't have to be constantly getting new toys."

"... Thanks?" Caleb said.

"You will be thankful, don't worry. I'm not concerned about that." The sheik beckoned Ibrahim to the table. "Take something to eat, Ibrahim. Then take the girl with you and get her accustomed to the work she will be doing."

"Yes, Your Highness," Ibrahim replied, filling up a plate and glancing at me.

I quickly filled my plate as well.

Caleb stood and pulled back my chair as I got to my feet. He glared at the sheik, then Ibrahim, then grabbed me by the back of the head and pressed his lips fiercely to mine.

"Done marking your territory, boy, or did you want to piss on her, too?" Ibrahim asked, rolling his eyes.

The sheik cleared his throat angrily. "None of that kind of talk, Ibrahim. That was very rude. Caleb, sit down. We have much to discuss. Jacey, go with Ibrahim."

I picked up my plate and followed Ibrahim, glancing back at Caleb. "Be good," I said.

"I will," Caleb grumbled.

The sheik's laughter followed Ibrahim and me down the long hall along the side of the gardens to a large, spacious office.

Ibrahim gestured to the smaller of two desks in the room. "That is your place."

"Yes, sir," I responded, going to the desk and setting my plate down. I was just about to sit at the computer there, when he cleared his throat.

"You will remove your dress," he ordered me.

I stared at him. "And wear… what?"

"The thong will be sufficient," he said.

"You… want me to work for you… naked?" I gaped.

He smirked. "Very much so. But I will let you keep the thong on."

The thong barely covered anything. I bit my lip, looking down at the dress I was wearing, then at him. "No?"

"No is not an option," he replied flatly. He snapped his fingers at me. "Take the dress off or I will cut it off you, and you will have to return to your room naked. Then what will Caleb think?"

This man was diabolical. "I..."

"Look but don't touch," Ibrahim reminded me.

I made a distressed sound in my throat.

Unmoved, he grabbed a letter opener off his desk.

Quickly, I pushed the dress off my shoulders and shimmied it to the floor.

"Better," he said, licking his lips as he looked at me.

I folded my arms over my breasts, trying to hide some of my nakedness from him.

"Ah, no. I get to see whatever I want." He pointed to my chair. "Go ahead and sit down. We will be covering a lot of ground today."

Shaking, I dropped my arms and hastily plopped myself behind the computer monitor to keep his eyes off me.

That only worked for a scant few seconds as Ibrahim came around the back of the desk and leaned over me. "Go ahead and turn it on," he breathed against my neck.

I blushed and reached down, pressing the button on the tower that would fire up the computer.

"Good girl." He waited silently while I squirmed in my chair, trying to figure out how to get him to stop looking at my breasts.

As the desktop came up on the computer screen, he reached over me. I snatched my hand away just in time for him to take control of the mouse.

"American women are always so obsessed with being a pile of sticks," he informed me. "I prefer a woman who has a few curves in all the right places. You are a beautiful woman, Jacey."

I swallowed. "Thank you."

"You're welcome." He started pulling up different programs, slowly, his breath still warm on my neck.

Clammy goosebumps rose on my skin.

"We will both get used to this in time," he said. "Though I can't imagine a day when I will not want to see you naked. It is a terrible shame the sheik has a soft spot for your boyfriend, or we would be on top of my desk now."

"I guess I should be thankful to the sheik, then," I murmured.

He raised an eyebrow at me.

"I-I mean, it's not that you're a bad-looking man, I just..." I stuttered.

"You just love Caleb. Well, someday the sheik will get tired of looking and want to touch. And when he is finished, he will let me touch. And then we will enjoy each other thoroughly." He smiled at me. "But, since today is not that day, I suppose you would like to learn more about our operations?"

"That would... probably be best," I agreed.

He nodded and showed me about a dozen spreadsheets and a sophisticated payroll system. "The sheik owns several legitimate businesses along with his other endeavors. You will learn about all of them. We will start with the oil because that is where most of his fortune comes from. Then, we will move on to trafficking."

"Human trafficking?" I asked, hoping it was something else.

"Yes. And drugs. And arms. The sheik has many varied interests," he said.

I nodded and turned back to the screen, ignoring his breath on my neck and shoulder as he showed me administrative duties. True to his word, he did not touch me.

But I still felt dirty when I went back to our room at the end of the day.

THE TWO ASSISTANTS

-Caleb-

The sheik let me finish dinner then brought me to his large, opulent office. There was an assistant's desk in one corner, which he showed me to, and it had a window behind it, which was nice. The window looked out on rolling fields of yellow flowers. There were a couple of old-fashioned windmills in the distance. A truly idyllic seen in a not quite so idyllic situation.

It turned out that doing work for the sheik wasn't all that different from doing work for Masterson. He even praised my work, amazed at how quickly I picked it up.

I wasn't exactly thrilled to be coordinating human trafficking again, but if that was the cost to save my life, and especially Jacey's, I wasn't going to turn it down.

"Now, I have several files on the different topics we discussed regarding Masterson's business," he said to me. "I want you to look them over and see if you remember anything else that needs to be added."

"Yes, sir," I replied, trying to sound as eager as I could.

The sheik just laughed and tousled my hair. "It's so funny that you fake enthusiasm so poorly. Maybe I should have you work naked like your girlfriend."

My blood froze in my veins. "Excuse me?!"

"It might be fun to see you squirm." The sheik shrugged.

"Go back to the part where Jacey is working naked?" I growled. Bile burned in my throat at the idea of Jacey being ogled by Ibrahim, and, to some extent, the sheik himself. She must have felt so vulnerable.

"Look but don't touch. Don't worry about it. Ibrahim is a stickler about rules. He will not disobey my order. But she is awfully lovely to look at. I think I will visit his office more often." He raised a challenging eyebrow at me. "Are you planning to make a fuss? I don't mind punishing those who make a fuss. I think you both enjoy being alive and unscathed, yes?"

My expression must have telegraphed the darkness of my thoughts because the sheik leaned in and settled his palms on my desktop, his face serious. "I won't tolerate insubordination, Caleb."

"Then maybe you should allow Jacey to wear—"

"*No* insubordination, Caleb. Consider carefully," he murmured dangerously. His eyebrows were drawn down in a deep scowl, and he leaned in close to me.

I set my teeth.

"It might not even be you I punish for it," he added.

That got me back on track. "Yes, sir," I seethed.

"Good boy," he said.

He might as well have said, 'Good dog.'

"I don't suppose it would do any good to politely ask you not to have my lover working naked?" I tried. It was a weak, last-ditch effort, I knew, but I was not above begging on Jacey's behalf.

"Not the slightest bit of good," he chortled. "Now, to those documents. I want you to really look at them and shake out all the cobwebs in your brain. See what you may have missed."

"Yes, sir." I opened the documents he pointed out to me.

It was a long day's work, and I did, indeed, remember more details, but finally I was able to return to our suite. Jacey was already there, sitting on the bed, back in her dress and pretending for all the world as though she hadn't just been admin-ing naked.

I decided I hated that dress. And that she was never going to wear it again.

"Caleb?" Jacey asked, her voice vulnerable as I stared at the barely-there clothing she wore.

I stalked over to her and ripped the flimsy thing right down the front. Doubtless, even though it was hardly a dress, it had been expensive. At least, I hoped it was.

"Caleb!" she gasped, bouncing back on the bed as I tore the rest of the dress off her. The thong she wore came next, snapped at both hips. Her lower lip trembled. "Are you mad at me?"

My heart softened, and I felt bad for scaring her. I pulled her up against me and kissed her, framing her face with my hands. "Baby, I'm not mad at you. I'm mad at them and what they're making you do."

"It's not a big deal. Just some computer work," she gulped, but I kissed the lie off her lips.

"Naked. They're having you do computer work naked," I said.

Jacey's whole body flushed. "I got to wear my underwear?"

"That's barely underwear." I pressed my forehead into her shoulder and took a couple of deep breaths.

"Would it... help if we had sex?" she asked tentatively.

I regarded her for a second. Her eyes were wide and vulnerable. She wanted to pretend for a while that everything was okay. I did, too. "Yes. A lot."

She unbuttoned my shirt and pushed it open, running her hands over my chest. "It's okay. He didn't touch me. Only you get to do that." She took my hand and kissed it, then laid it over her breast before getting to work on my belt.

My hands joined hers at my belt and worked it open. My fly was next, and then we only bothered shoving my pants down enough for my straining cock to spring free.

Jacey widened her legs and, seeing she was already glistening wet for me, I lined myself up and pushed inside her.

We both groaned.

"Baby, you feel so good," I murmured in her ear as I started to thrust. Possessively.

She rocked on the bed, taking all of me, wrapping her legs around my waist. "More, Caleb," she begged. "Give me more. Make me yours again."

"Fuck yes," I agreed and rammed her hard, my balls slapping against her wet skin.

Jacey gripped my shoulders and threw her head back, and her inner muscles began to milk my cock as she came.

The first time.

Though it was agony to resist, I needed to put my stamp on this woman. I pounded her until we were both sweaty and breathless.

"Caleb, oh my God..." she moaned.

"Just keep on coming for me, baby," I murmured. "Let me feel it around my dick."

She clung to me, her whole body shaking now, her teeth chattering as orgasm after orgasm rocked through her.

On the crest of her next orgasm, I finally came as well, shoving myself as deep into her as I could go as I jetted into her.

We collapsed together in a tangle of limbs, both completely spent.

"How are we going to face tomorrow?" Jacey asked half an hour later as she laid on my chest.

I knew reality would have to intrude eventually. I'd just wished we had more time. "I don't like them looking at you naked," I replied gruffly, tracing circles on her back with my fingertips.

"I don't think we have a whole lot of choice in the matter," she said, sounding miserable. "It's... creepy. Like that old man at the logging camp. I mean, when is he going to start 'accidentally' brushing my boob with his arm and stuff like that?"

"He'd better not." I sounded very growly and unhappy, even to my own ears. "But that's not your fault." I moved my hand up to massage the base of her scalp.

She smoothed her hand over my nipple and certain places lower on my body began to perk up. "I wish we could just stay like this forever."

"Me, too," I said. Lying naked with Jacey was second only to being inside her.

"I don't want to go to sleep because, in the morning, we have to do it all over again," she whispered.

I stared at the ceiling, taking in the wood mosaic over my head. "I love you. I know that's probably not enough right now, but I'm afraid it's all I've got."

She cuddled into me more tightly. "It's enough."

To me, it wasn't. My love for her couldn't keep her safe, and it frustrated the hell out of me.

"Jacey, I..." I began.

The wooden shutters over our window suddenly exploded inward, littering us with shrapnel.

I rolled Jacey to the floor on instinct and laid on top of her, shielding her with my body from whatever might come next.

There was the rat-tat-tat of automatic weapons fire and bullets buried themselves in the stone and tile of the walls, but luckily most of it happened above us, though I did feel a hot zing across my back.

"Fuck!" I muttered.

"Caleb, are you okay?" Jacey asked.

"Just a graze, I think," I said through gritted teeth. "What the fuck is going on around here?!"

"I don't know." She sounded as scared as I felt.

But the two of us didn't need to be panicking. "Let's get to the door. If we can get out of here, maybe we'll be safe."

I had no fucking clue if getting out of the room would be better or worse, but I needed to give us both some kind of hope. Between gunshots, I rolled off Jacey and began army-crawling to the door. She did the same.

We were just getting close enough to reach up and grab the handle, when the door swung open.

A masked man with an automatic weapon strode in wearing combat boots, gear, and a balaclava.

Then another, much more familiar man in a suit came in behind him, straightening his jacket.

"You are *such* a pain in my ass," Masterson said.

"Fuck." I couldn't think of anything else to say.

The man in combat gear reached down and yanked me up by my hair. "Don't make me do the girl," he growled.

I didn't know in which context he meant it, but either way, I didn't like it. I went still in his grip, completely compliant.

"Good boy." Masterson turned and the guy began to march me out of the room.

"What about Jacey?" I asked.

"You don't deserve Jacey," Masterson growled. "Maybe when you're gone, the sheik or his lackey will take… good care of her."

That was when I started to struggle. "I won't let you separate us!"

"Watch me." Masterson nodded to the man and then I felt a sting in my neck.

"What did you…?"

It was the last thing I said.

ALONE WITH IBRAHIM

-Jacey-

I lay, sprawled on my stomach as Masterson dragged Caleb away, unable to do anything to stop him.

"No..." I whispered.

Gunfire stopped coming into the bedroom and moved off to a different location within the hacienda.

I couldn't move. I just stayed in the same spot on the floor, stunned.

Caleb was gone.

It seemed like hours, but it may only have been minutes, until the gunfire stopped altogether.

Then I saw a pair of shoes shuffle in front of the doorway.

"So they left us one," the sheik said.

"Interesting." Another pair of shoes. Ibrahim.

"I suppose we'll have to change locations now. Damn Masterson anyway," the sheik grunted.

"But we'll still have her," Ibrahim said.

"Indeed. All right, Jacey, let's go." The sheik waited.

When I didn't move right away, Ibrahim grabbed me firmly by the hair and hauled me to my feet.

It was then that I became acutely aware that I was still naked.

"I-I need to get some clothes," I said, crossing my arms over my breasts.

"No, you don't," the sheik replied. "You belong to Ibrahim now. If you ever wear clothes again, it will be at his discretion."

Ibrahim smiled slightly.

"No!" I protested, trying to twist away, but his grip was iron.

"Put a robe on her, and let's get her in the car. I hope Cordoba is nice this time of year," the sheik said, turning away.

"Where's Caleb?" I asked, even though I was sure I already knew the answer.

"Gone. With Masterson. You should start thinking about yourself now," Ibrahim responded. He dragged me back into the room and threw me on the bed.

The sheik clucked his tongue. "There's no time for that now, Ibrahim. Masterson's goons are still mowing down my guards."

"I know. I'm just grabbing her a robe," he said. He threw open the wardrobe and grabbed a robe, tossing it onto the bed next to me. "Put it on."

Shakily, I got up and pulled on the robe, cinching it in the middle. "We're going to Cordoba?" I asked.

"Yes," the sheik said.

"Where are we now?" I followed up my question with another.

"Toledo. Now let's go before the authorities get here." The sheik spun on his heel, and we hurried through the bullet-riddled hacienda to a large side garage.

The sheik's staff were already frantically packing things into black SUVs. Ibrahim brought me to a black town car and shoved me in the back seat. "Behave," he said. "Or you're going to regret it."

I was sure he meant it. I sat still, trying to work out how I might get out of the town car once we were underway and get to the authorities the sheik was talking about. Maybe Masterson and Caleb were still in the country, and they'd be able to locate them if they knew to be looking.

After Ibrahim closed the door, I subtly tried the door handle on my side. It didn't budge.

Or not so subtly.

He opened the other door again. "Jacey, I told you to be good," he warned.

I sprang into a sitting-straight-up position, folding my hands between my knees. "I had to check," I said.

"Of course you did," he snorted.

The sheik then got in the back next to me. "It's nice to have such a lovely travel companion, at least," he grinned as Ibrahim got into the passenger seat, and then a driver got in and got us underway.

I smiled weakly, trying not to shudder when he put his hand on my knee.

"Don't worry, precious. Ibrahim will have you wondering who this Caleb person was in less than a week," he said confidently.

"I don't want to forget Caleb. And I won't forget him," I replied stubbornly.

The sheik patted my knee before settling his hand back down and rubbing it. "Of course not. You never forget your first time, or your first love."

"He will be my first and last of both," I assured him.

With a loud guffaw, the sheik patted my knee again, spreading my robe so he was touching my skin. "You just keep telling yourself that."

"I will." I stared mutinously out the window, trying to ignore the hand on my knee and the hungry look that had been in the sheik's eyes.

"You did tell her she would be mine, did you not?" Ibrahim asked, turning around and raising an eyebrow at the sheik.

The sheik sighed, and blessedly, took his hand away. "You're right, Ibrahim. I did say that. For services rendered. You saved my life and asked only for the girl in return. It's the least I can do. She's just so… delicious."

"I'm sure she will be," Ibrahim smirked before turning back to the front.

Images of Ibrahim sweating on top of me while he took advantage of me, ignoring my protests and my attempts to fend him off, filled my mind. I squeezed my eyes shut, willing them away.

"Can I just have a little eye candy for the road?" the sheik asked, licking his lips.

Ibrahim did not look back again. He simply nodded.

The sheik undid the silk belt at my waist and spread the robe open while I determinedly pretended it wasn't happening, and it didn't bother me. I wasn't going to give them the satisfaction of seeing me break down.

"Marvelous," the sheik breathed. "Simply stunning. That Caleb, selfish bastard, keeping all this for himself."

"It is a shame," Ibrahim agreed. "But now we have her and, without him arguing all the time, we can be more free with our... needs. I will tire of her eventually, I'm sure."

"Then it's a good thing I have such a nice, big bed," the sheik said.

I huffed. "Are you two *quite* done? You're not going to scare me, and you're not going to touch me."

"How do you think you're going to enforce that edict?" the sheik chortled while Ibrahim laughed as well.

I had no idea, but I wasn't going to tell them that. "You'll see," was all I could come up with at the moment.

The two men laughed harder, and even the driver joined in.

"What are you going to do? Start carving 'God will grant me justice' into the walls of Ibrahim's bedroom when he locks you in there?" the sheik asked.

"You know how that movie ended?" I said.

"No. I don't remember. Why don't you tell me?" the sheik chuckled.

I finally turned and looked at him. "Not well for the people who wronged Edmond Dantes."

"Oh-ho! Now she's threatening us!" The sheik doubled over, laughing.

"It's cute," Ibrahim smirked.

"It's adorable," the sheik agreed.

I pursed my lips and looked back out the window, simmering inside.

They tried to needle me several more times during the car ride to Cordoba, but I remained determinedly silent. They weren't going to get another rise out of me.

Besides, I was busy praying for a miracle.

We must have reached Cordoba, but one wouldn't have known it because, instead of entering the city, we were outside it once again in an hacienda-style compound. I pulled my robe closed again and got out of the car as soon as the driver unlocked the doors.

"Jacey, you're with me," Ibrahim barked, beckoning me with a snap of his fingers.

Like a dog.

Still, I held my head high as I walked with Ibrahim. He led me to a large room with an attached office. And one bed.

"So," I asked primly, "where will you be staying?"

Ibrahim just laughed. "Oh, princess. You are delightful. Take off your robe."

I doubled down and folded my arms across it instead.

He cocked his head to one side. "If you want your shot at getting back to Caleb, I would expect you would need to be alive and mobile to do it."

I swallowed and quickly undid my robe, letting it fall to the floor.

"Excellent. We have work to do today that will last long into the evening. I might not get around the fucking you today, but believe me, it will be soon." Ibrahim waved me toward the office.

Stiffly, I walked into the office and found my secretarial desk in the corner by the window. It was very similar to the one we'd just abandoned back in Toledo.

"Now," he said, leaning over me as I started up my tower, "do you remember all your logins and passwords?"

"Yes," I replied tersely.

As I expected, the back of his hand 'accidentally' brushed my nipple when he reached for the mouse. I didn't give him the satisfaction of a response.

"I need you to categorize these expenses, just like you were doing back at the other compound," he said, his breath fanning the baby hairs on the back of my neck.

It surprised me that they didn't stand straight up as my skin crawled. "All right. But you know, we drove through the night and I haven't slept—"

"That you were fucking Caleb instead of sleeping before the incursion is not my problem," Ibrahim snapped. "Unless you'd like to go to bed right now."

"Of course I'd like to go to bed right now!" I grumped.

"With me." He raised an eyebrow in challenge.

Shit. "You know what? These numbers are truly fascinating. I think I'll work to catch up."

"I thought you might," he chuckled. "I need to meet with the sheik, but I know you're not going to do anything stupid. You're locked out of the internet and e-mail systems. There's really nothing you can do."

"You know I'm going to try," I told him.

"I know. I find it entertaining that you continue to think there's a way out for you. Or Caleb." He shook his head. "You're both in it too deep now. The best you can hope for is that, one of these days, when we trade or sell you, you end up in the same place."

That was not heartening to hear. I wanted out. So did Caleb. "We'll see."

"I'm sure we will," he replied. Then he stood, dropped a kiss on the top of my head, and left the suite.

As I promised, I tried everything I knew to get the computer to send out a distress call, but nothing worked. Not that there was much for me to try. I was no hacker.

Finally, I resigned myself to the work in front of me and worked all day while Ibrahim was gone.

Servants came in and out with food, so I didn't dare put my robe back on. I simply worked and munched on croissant rolls and salads. In the evening, I got paella.

True to his word, Ibrahim did not return to the suite until very late. "You can stop working now," he said, yawning. "You and I need to get some sleep before tomorrow. It's going to be a big day."

"I'm not having sex with you," I blurted, crossing my arms over my chest.

"Not tonight, no. But tomorrow, I think I can make time." He smiled, and it seemed to have a touch of evil to it. "Now, get in the bed."

"Naked?!" I gaped.

"Yes. Naked." He stabbed his finger at the bed. "Get in."

I haltingly went to the bed, remembering his threat about being alive and mobile if I wanted to figure a way out of my situation. I got under the covers and pulled the bedding around me like a cocoon.

He just laughed. "I'm going to need some blankets, too."

"Then go get some," I replied mutinously.

"Hmm. No." He stripped naked before me, slowly.

I turned my face into the pillow. I didn't want to watch another man undress.

"Look at me," he ordered. "Or I'll make time tonight."

Turning onto my back, I watched as Ibrahim finished undressing. All the way.

He had a semi, and I was disgusted.

"Are you happy now?" I asked as he got into bed next to me.

Ibrahim pulled on the covers and disturbed my cocoon. He lay on his back next to me, our arms touching, skin-to-skin. "Not yet," he murmured, yawning again. "But trust me. I will be tomorrow."

THE DOUBLE-CROSS

-Caleb-

As usual, Masterson was pissed at me so I got to ride in the trunk with the spare digging into my side. There was a thin carpet between me and the tire, so at least I wouldn't get a burn from the rubber rolling along my naked skin. But it certainly wasn't comfortable.

I was panicking about Jacey. I hoped she was alive. I wondered whose hands she had fallen into or if she was still with that asshole of a pervert the sheik. Ibrahim was just as bad, if not worse. Making her work naked. What a load of crap.

The car bumped along cobblestone at some point. Not sure if it was necessary or just Masterson's plan to have me all bruised up by the time we reached our destination. Most of the trip was highway, as far as I could feel.

Eventually, the car stopped, and the trunk opened. Harsh halogen lighting pierced the darkness. "Caleb, you made it," Masterson grinned.

"I'm not going anywhere without Jacey," I reiterated. It would have sounded more threatening if I hadn't been bound hand and foot at the time.

Masterson laughed, of course. "Ah, Caleb, you always are a stitch.

Brandon, pick up our little friend here and get him on the jet. I'm missing a nice port and a good steak."

Brandon, who I thought I recognized by his build as the man who had originally separated Jacey and me, hefted me out of the trunk and up over his shoulder.

I started to flop around like a fish.

"Do you want to be put out again?" Brandon growled.

I stopped flopping. "No."

"Good. Then knock it off." Brandon walked after Masterson up the steps of the jet and into the body of the plane. He dumped me in a leather chair and buckled my lap belt. "Stay," he commanded.

Like I was a dog.

Masterson sat, and despite my highest hopes, no one stopped the jet from taking off. The brightly-lit tarmac disappeared further and further into darkness as the plane lifted into the air. I looked at the sparkle of lights below that was soon all that was left of Spain. Jacey was somewhere down there, and I had no idea what was happening to her.

I looked around desperately, my mind even considering parachuting out if I could find one. And get out of my bonds. Those were two really big 'ifs,' neither of which seemed very likely at the moment.

Leather stuck to my skin as I started to sweat. I tried shifting in my seat, but that just made the situation worse. The leather pulled at my flesh, making sticky sounds every time I moved and causing a sting in the process.

While in flight, Masterson had his steak and port. He didn't offer me anything, of course. I probably would have spit it in his face anyway. I was still naked, and bound, and I didn't have Jacey. That put me in a mood, to say the least.

"Ah," he said, dabbing his mouth with a cloth napkin once he was finished. "As I was saying, Caleb. You are such a pain in the ass."

"I'd hate to disappoint you," I quipped back.

"Indeed." He laid his napkin down. "So, what did you tell the sheik?"

"Everything." I didn't bother lying. I was actually still a bit proud of my little rebellion.

Masterson pressed his lips together in a thin line. "I must say, I am disappointed, Caleb. But, I suppose it's a blessing in disguise. Now you can tell me everything you know about his operations."

I laughed. "You nabbed the wrong one, then. Jacey was working for Ibrahim."

"Oh, but I think you still learned a lot. You were with the sheik all evening. Unless he changed sexual preferences since I last saw him, I'm sure he was teaching you things about the business." Masterson folded his arms over his chest. "Come now, Caleb. We know each other well enough not to bullshit each other."

I grimaced. "I'm not telling you shit. The sheik still has Jacey. Or someone else has her. Or whatever. But she's not here, is she? I could be putting her in danger by running my mouth to you."

"Brandon?" he said in an offhand kind of way.

Brandon came over and smacked me across the face. My head snapped to the side and I briefly saw stars before my senses sharpened and I tasted blood in my mouth.

"Now then. You were saying?" Masterson encouraged.

I spat blood, hitting Brandon's boot. That made me smile. "I was saying you can go fuck yourself."

"Hmm. Sorry, not the response I'm looking for." He nodded to Brandon.

Brandon hit me again, so hard my ears rang. It hurt now, but I was going to look and feel like hell in the morning.

I didn't care.

"Let's try this again, shall we?" Masterson said.

"You can try," I replied, feeling my eye swell up. It throbbed painfully, sending an answering drumbeat through my head and causing one hell of a headache. "But you're not going to get anywhere. You should have grabbed Jacey when you had the chance."

"But then, how would I punish you?" he replied reasonably.

"Dunno. You planning to put splinters under my fingernails next?" I asked.

I could just hear Jacey shouting in my head. *Don't give him ideas!*

"Unfortunately, I don't have any splinters with me, but we can try that when we get home," Masterson grinned.

"Lucky me," I responded.

"Oh no. Lucky *me*. I haven't tried that one before, and I've been so looking forward to seeing how effective it is." He smiled at the flight attendant who came to clear his dinner setting. "Thank you, Sheila."

She blushed. "You're welcome, Mr. Masterson."

"Would you like to join me in the mile high club again?" he asked politely, as though ordering a second drink.

Sheila fluffed her hair. "I'd love to, Mr. Masterson."

"See, Caleb?" he said, not taking his eyes off her as he crooked his finger at her and then patted his lap. "This is what a good, willing employee does."

"Good for her," I replied.

She pulled up her skirt and shimmied out of her panties, then opened Masterson's fly before settling herself down on his cock.

I wrinkled my nose in disgust and turned away. Brandon watched the scene with interest as bodies slapped together and wet noises and moans filled the air.

"Not as into watching as I am, are you, Caleb?" Masterson chuckled.

"No," I responded.

"Too bad. I might have asked you to join in. If you'd been good," he said.

I could tell they were reaching the end because the sounds sped up and Sheila started making loud, clearly fake sounds of pleasure.

Masterson didn't seem to care, though. He grunted, and I decided he was finished.

I turned back just in time to see him shove her off his lap.

"Go get cleaned up," he muttered, waving a hand. "Then, I want a martini."

"Yes, Mr. Masterson," she replied obediently and went to the back of the jet where, I assumed, there was a bathroom.

"Now, where were we? Ah yes. The sheik," he said, glancing at

Brandon. "You know, if you prove to be more trouble than you're worth, I can always do to you what I did to Hank."

I froze.

"Then you wouldn't be having any more fun with Jacey ever again. Even if you could get her back," he pointed out.

Brandon cracked his knuckles as though ready to break my spine right then and there.

But still, I thought of Jacey and hesitated.

"I think this time at the neck. We only need him to be able to talk, after all," Masterson mused.

With a grim smile, Brandon flipped open a switchblade.

"Fine!" I said. Jacey and I wouldn't do much escaping together if I was a quadriplegic.

"That's better," Masterson beamed.

Brandon looked almost disappointed as he put his knife away.

"What do you want to know?" I asked, wiping my mouth against my shoulder. It was still bleeding.

"Everything, Caleb," he said. "I want to know everything. But not now. We'll get to the dirty details when we're back home."

Home. That place was never going to be my home.

Masterson settled back in his chair and closed his eyes. "It's been a long night. I suggest you get some sleep, Caleb. You'll be, how did you put it? 'Running your mouth'? All day tomorrow. It's going to be pretty tiring."

I narrowed my eyes at him, but he just drifted off into a blissful, untroubled sleep. The sleep of someone who did bad things and didn't give a damn about it.

"I'd do as he says," Brandon suggested. "It's a long flight."

I eyeballed him suspiciously, then closed my eyes, trying to ignore the throbbing pain in my face and my attacker at my side. After all, Masterson was the devil I knew. There was some comfort in that. Not as much comfort as there would have been if Jacey had been there with me, but some.

When I woke, the plane had landed, and Masterson was still

asleep. Brandon heaved me up onto his shoulder again, and this time I didn't struggle.

He walked me down the steps of the jet to another nondescript black town car. I imagined Masterson was right behind us.

Only I didn't hear footfalls. Or voices.

"Back in the trunk you go," Brandon grunted, opening the trunk and tossing me in like a sack of potatoes.

My elbow hit hard on something metal and I was certain I'd just gotten rug burn on my hip, but I bit back a yelp. I wasn't going to give him the satisfaction.

Still no footfalls. "Where's everyone else?" I asked. "Where's the envoy?"

"Just you and me for now, kid," he replied. "I suggest you get used to it."

I stared at him. "What? Just you and me? What the hell is going on now?!"

Brandon just grinned.

And slammed the trunk shut, leaving me in the dark.

A DAY OUT

-Jacey-

When I woke up, Ibrahim was not in bed, and that gave me an infinite sense of relief.

I sat up, holding the sheet up over my chest just in case he was still in the room.

A low chuckle emanated from the office. "It's adorable that you think you're going to get away with that. Go ahead and go shower. Then we have work to do," Ibrahim said.

With an angry blush, I yanked the sheet free of the mattress and wore it around me to the bathroom. Ibrahim's laughter followed behind me.

I slammed the door shut then took stock of what was to be had in the bathroom. There was a robe, but it was so big it was clearly for Ibrahim. There was not another robe for me. No surprise there.

In the shower, there were all manner of soaps, shampoos, and conditioners on a built-in ledge. It was a modern zero level entry tile shower bigger than most walk-in closets, with shower heads and jets and handles galore.

I just went for the simple waterfall function and washed with something that smelled like vanilla. Then I stepped out, dried off, brushed my hair, and marched back into the bedroom in a towel.

"Not the rules, Jacey," Ibrahim said absently.

I wondered how he could even see me without turning around, then I caught the edge of his screen and saw there was a camera feed there of the bedroom and bathroom. Of course.

Muttering under my breath, I tossed the towel back in the bathroom and padded stark naked into the office.

"Better," he said, finally looking up. He did a slow once-over of my assets then waved a hand in the direction of my desk. "I e-mailed you a list of tasks. It should take you until this afternoon. Then, we're going into Cordoba."

"We're… going into the city?" I gaped, completely thrown. "And… I thought you said my e-mail wouldn't work?"

"We have an internal network. Your e-mail won't e-mail *outside* of the network," he clarified. "And yes, we're going into the city. So I expect you to be on your best behavior."

Screw that. The second we got into the city, I was going to create such a ruckus that it'd bring all of Interpol down on us and this place. I just smiled and nodded, though. He didn't need to know my plans.

"And if you're thinking of making a fuss once we get there, please keep in mind I can snap your neck like a twig in seconds, and it's a Moorish city. There are all kinds of twists and turns and alleys I can drag you down to shut you up," he said in an offhanded sort of way.

Damn.

I decided I'd take in the lay of the land once we got there and then make a plan. I went to my desk and sat down, getting everything up and running before opening the e-mail he'd sent me. He was right. This was going to take me well into the afternoon to finish.

While working, Ibrahim was very professional. He dipped in and out of the office, presumably going to see the sheik, while servants brought me food and I remained at my desk.

The last time he returned, Ibrahim brought a T-shirt, underwear, jeans, and flat sandals with him. "I can't very well bring you into town naked," he explained.

It felt like I'd just had seven Christmases at once, and I ran to grab the clothes.

He 'accidentally' brushed my nipple again when handing them over then started getting changed himself into something more casual than I'd ever seen him wear.

I got dressed in record time, a little miffed that he hadn't brought a bra, but I wasn't about to complain. At least, in this warm weather, I wasn't going to start nipping out. I hoped.

Two minutes later, we were in a black sedan with a driver I'd come to recognize. He kept glancing in the rearview mirror at me and giving little smiles until Ibrahim grunted a warning. Then he kept his eyes on the road.

We were dropped off on a cobblestone street. Ibrahim put an arm around me, and it was like a vice, though to those passing by, we likely looked like just another happy couple on a romantic getaway. Maybe with the woman having a bout of motion sickness.

"Smile a little. Take in the sights," he said, putting his mouth right by my ear. "It might be the only opportunity you get to see this part of the world."

I forced a smile that was probably more of a grimace and began looking around me, taking in the streets that disappeared around corners, the whitewashed walls, and window boxes.

Ibrahim brought me to a place labeled 'La Mezquita.' "This is the largest mosque in Spain," he said proudly. "Of course, it's a conglomeration of cultures. It was built on a site already being used for another religion's purposes—probably pagan—then the Catholic Church took it over later and built a chapel right in the middle. But I think you'll find it impressive."

I was prepared to turn up my nose at whatever he was about to show me as we walked inside with the rest of the tourists, but unfortunately, I was actually impressed. Awestricken, really.

There were what looked like miles and miles of Arabic arches, striped orange and white, held up by columns. Every corridor of them seemed to disappear before you could see the end of it.

Ibrahim explained the differences in the columns, saying, like many cultures do, the Moors cannibalized Greek and Roman architecture for columns to use within the mosque, as well as making some of their own.

I felt like I had my own personal tour guide. It was so overwhelming, I almost forgot I was a prisoner.

"What are we doing here?" I asked.

"Making a deal," he replied. "It's a good place for it. All kinds of corners and columns to hide around."

"Huh." I looked around as we went by some side chapels the Church had built once It had taken over the mosque, complete with barred gates that could be closed and locked if necessary. That was more of a reminder of my prison situation. "So, then, why am I here?"

He just smiled slightly and steered me into one chapel that had a painting of Christ on the cross at the back of it. There was one other person inside, kneeling at the kneeler.

Ibrahim forced me to kneel down next to him. "Max," he said.

"Ibrahim," Max replied. "I see you brought the goods."

I looked around, trying to see what Ibrahim had brought. Then I realized 'the goods' was me. "Oh fuck," I groaned.

"Now, now, Jacey, you're in a holy space," Ibrahim admonished me while Max chuckled.

I pressed my forehead to the wooden bar of the kneeler and let out a cry of frustration. "What about the sheik?" I asked.

"I've decided it would be best for me to go my own way," Ibrahim said. "As such, I thought I'd get myself a little seed money for my own operations. And you are just so deliciously valuable these days, Jacey." He sighed. "So terribly unfortunate I didn't get to sample you, but the deal was clearly laid out that I couldn't, or I'd be giving you away at a hefty discount."

I looked over at Max. He looked every inch an American tourist, even holding a baseball cap in his hand as he was not allowed to wear it in the holy space. "So, who the he-heck are you, and where am I going now?"

Max smiled and stood, taking me by the arm as he took out his phone.

Ibrahim had his in his hand already.

Each phone let out a tiny beep, and Ibrahim tucked his back in his pocket. "Nice doing business with you," he said.

"Likewise," Max replied. "Good luck. Catch you later."

"I very much doubt that, but we'll see how it goes." Ibrahim dropped a kiss on the top of my head, smelled my hair, then walked out of the chapel.

"So?" I prompted Max again.

"You know, this is the Chapel of the Souls of Purgatory," he mused aloud. "It makes me think of you and Caleb."

I stiffened. "You know Caleb?"

"Not yet. But I'm going to," he replied.

That was some comfort, at least. "So, we're going to be together again."

"Oh yes," he said. "Very soon."

Okay. I could survive whatever hell was next for us as long as Caleb was there. "Go ahead and take me to him," I acquiesced.

He smiled and gestured for me to walk ahead of him out of the chapel and back into La Mezquita proper. Then he guided me out of the mosque (the place was so big I wouldn't have been surprised if I'd gotten lost) and out onto the street.

We walked back to where another nondescript black sedan was waiting to pick us up.

"Um," I asked nervously as I got in the back. "Who do I have to thank for getting me away from the sheik and bringing me back to Caleb?"

Max didn't reply until the door closed behind him, and all the tinted windows were up. As we got underway, he reached under the Hawaiian shirt he had over a T-shirt and fished for something. I could see the handle of a gun in a shoulder strap.

I swallowed.

Then he produced a leather wallet. "Here," he said, handing it to me.

I flipped it open and saw, it was not a wallet, but a badge! "Seriously?!" I all but shrieked with excitement. "I was going to scream my head off to see if I could get the attention of the police, and I was just thinking of Interpol when we came to Cordoba, but this is so much better!"

Max, the CIA agent, grinned at me. "Sorry to cut your vacation short, but I thought you might just want to go home."

"Yeah, I'd love to!" Then I bit my lip. "But I'm not… I mean, aside from the United States, I'm not sure where home is anymore."

"Well, it's WitSec again. I'm not sure where they're putting you up this time, but it'll go much better than the last time," he assured me. "They found the mole in the FBI who ratted you out and got your agent killed."

Poor Darren. I hoped they fried the bastard who caused his death. "Good. I hope they send him to the gas chamber or something."

He laughed. "Who said he was going to make it to trial?"

"Even better," I said grimly. "So, we're flying back to Minnesota?"

"No. I can't actually tell you where we're going, but you might recognize it when we get there. You might not," he responded. "I'm not even sure you'll be staying where I'm taking you for the hand-off. Probably not. They're quite interested in making sure you two make it to trial. Then Interpol wants a piece so back to Europe at some point. This could take years."

"Years?" I sighed.

"Years. The wheels of justice move slowly, especially when people like Masterson and the sheik pay people off to make them grind to a halt." He didn't look happy about that. "It's really frustrating as an agent of the law to see all your hard work gumming up like that."

I nodded, understanding. "I really want to get them both now. And that squad of assassins who had me."

"The Triumvirate," he said. "When we catch them, and we will catch them, we'll probably call you back as a witness again. They had you and not Caleb, right?"

"Right," I confirmed.

"I'll make note of that in my mission report. I'm glad this all hasn't scared you off being a witness." He gave me an impressed look.

I folded my arms over my chest. "If anything, it's just pissed me off more and made me more eager to stick it to them. All of them."

"Good," he said. "Because there are at least sixteen different agencies all over the face of the globe hoping you can do just that."

THE HAND-OFF

-Caleb-

I was getting tired of trunks. Fed up to my eyeballs, really. Exactly how many times and by how many nefarious organizations could a person reasonably be expected to be kidnapped? I was sure Jacey and I were approaching some kind of record.

Jacey.

My stomach churned at the thought of having left her in the crossfire at the sheik's hacienda. Was she okay? Was she with the sheik?

Maybe Masterson had just punked me and had sent someone to go grab Jacey after. A man could hope.

After a long stretch of what I would have called highway, by the feel of it, we were suddenly bumping along worse than on the cobblestone in Spain. I rolled around the trunk, knowing I was getting the ever-loving hell bruised out of me, but not able to do a whole lot about it.

One particularly deep rut actually made me hit the trunk lid.

We stopped shortly thereafter. I stifled a groan of pain. Maybe it was me trying to be a bit too manly, but I didn't want any of the sons of bitches having the satisfaction of knowing they'd hurt me.

The trunk lid popped open, and I looked up into a thousand stars. Then a flashlight beamed right in my face, and I winced reflexively.

"You *had* to bring him in the trunk?" a voice I didn't recognize asked. It was a woman, by the tone.

"It's more fun that way. Besides, they always ask inane questions when you take them in the back seat," Brandon replied. "And I hate telling people over and over that I don't know a damn thing."

"Still… oh, and you knocked him around a bit, too, I see," the woman sighed, poking her head into the light.

She was blonde, skinny, and dressed in a professional blouse and jacket. She shook her head as she looked down at me. "Brandon, Jesus, could you just once, *just once*, bring one of them to me in one piece?!"

"Um… hi, I'm Caleb?" I interjected.

"Yes, I know who you are," the woman replied testily.

"Bea, come on. It wouldn't be me if I didn't end up roughing them up a little. Besides, Masterson ordered it," Brandon said.

She let out a slow, seething breath. "Just get him in the house."

"No can do. Delivery stops at this point. He can still walk, though. I think. Well, I suppose if you undo the duct tape around his ankles," Brandon shrugged.

Her eyes narrowed on Brandon. "And if he can't? It's not like I can carry him, Brandon."

"That sounds like a you problem," he replied and took out his switchblade, none-too-carefully slitting the tape at my ankles.

"Hey! Careful with the merchandise!" Bea protested.

He put his knife away then grabbed me by the hair and dragged me out of the trunk. "Can you stand?" he grunted.

I wobbled as I got my feet under me, but I stood, naked and barefoot, in the middle of some woods. If I ever stopped being passed around like the bad guys were playing hot potato, I was never going camping again. I'd seen enough woods to last me a lifetime.

"Walk with me," she ordered, still glaring at Brandon. "I'll be reaching out to your superiors about this."

He just flipped her the bird then got back into the car and drove away.

"Fucker," she muttered. "Well, come along. We haven't got all night!"

"I can't see where I'm walking," I replied. "And I'm barefoot."

Bea paused then shined her own flashlight just ahead of both of us so I could see the ground where I was walking. "Better?"

"Much." I carefully walked with her down a long dirt-and-grass drive that curved around into the woods. It reminded me a little bit of the drive leading up to the safe house where Darren had died.

Poor Darren.

I wondered just how many fucking people I was going to lose by the time this ended and if one of them was going to be Jacey.

"You'll be staying here until the next team comes to get you," Bea said as we rounded the bend, and I saw a huge Adirondack-style cabin. The big A-line windows looked down upon the drive here. I didn't see any kind of lake, so I guessed the back windows looked out into the woods.

"Great. More woods," I grumbled.

"This is actually a senator's summer house, donated for the occasion. I'd be grateful, if I were you. I could have put you in a little cement box of a basement apartment," she snapped back.

"Oh, I'm sorry, Miss Bad Guy, I really should be more grateful," I snarked.

She stopped. "What makes you think I'm with the bad guys?"

"Aren't you?" I asked, suddenly unsure.

Bea tucked the flashlight under her arm and reached into her jacket pocket. She tossed me a leather wallet that I caught and curiously flipped open.

"You're FBI," I gaped.

She snatched her badge back. "Yes. Now if you wouldn't mind, I'd like to get that duct tape off of you and get to bed. We have a special solution so we don't rip your skin off, but it's in the house."

"I'm sorry about Darren," I said quietly as we walked up wooden steps to a long, wraparound deck. The door was centered in the middle of the house, excluding the garage that was connected off to the left. It must have been at least a four-car garage.

"Yes, well, he knew the risks," she sniffed, squaring her shoulders. She unlocked the door and opened it.

I saw movement at the perimeter, just inside the darkness not penetrated by the house's lights, and I froze. "I think we've got company," I whispered.

Bea touched her ear. "Dale, wave. You're scaring the kid."

A man with a big gun, wearing combat gear, stepped just into the light and waved. Then he stepped back into the darkness.

"Well-spotted, though. We don't get many who notice the perimeter guard. Which, of course, is the whole point," she said.

"I learned from experience to start checking my six," I replied.

"No doubt. All right, in we go." She held the door open, so I stepped inside first.

The cabin, or rather summer home, had an open floor plan. I saw two more agents sitting at the dining table off from the kitchen eating sandwiches.

"Egads, Bea, I thought he'd never get here!" one said around a mouthful of food.

"Chew and swallow, Mike," she answered. "And yeah, it feels like Brandon took the long way just so he could mess with the kid some more."

"He's a dick," the other man grunted.

She snorted. "No argument here. Okay, so, where's the anti-gummy solution? We've got to get this tape off him."

The men took a second look at me then. "He's naked," Mike observed.

"No shit," she said. "Ed? You know where the solution is?"

"Guest bathroom, top shelf of the medicine cabinet," he responded.

Bea nodded and led me into the living room. "Sit down," she said, pointing to a, thankfully, cloth-upholstered sofa. "I'll get the stuff and get you out of that duct tape."

"Thanks," I said, sitting down while she walked off. I took note of where the guest bathroom was because I was going to need it soon.

She returned shortly thereafter with a bottle, a small pair of scissors, and cotton swabs. "All right. If I do this right, this should be relatively painless."

"Sounds good. I'm sure Masterson was just planning to rip it off me when we got back to his place," I replied.

"I wouldn't be surprised." She cut the tape holding my wrists together so I could separate them at least, then got to work swabbing and peeling.

It didn't take long for her to remove the duct tape, and all that was left in its wake was a tiny bit of stickiness and some redness from them putting it on. Taking it off really hadn't hurt at all.

"Thanks," I said again.

"You're welcome. Now, I'd suggest hopping in the shower and then getting some sleep. We won't have movement again for another thirteen hours," she informed me. "Mike will lend you some clothes."

Mike spluttered around his sandwich. "Why me?"

"Because you're the right build, idiot." She rolled her eyes.

"Oh." Mike blushed at his stupid question.

Ed just started to laugh.

"Okay, you two knuckleheads. Let's get it together. You two taking first watch?" she asked.

It wasn't really a question.

"Yes, boss," Ed responded.

"Good." She motioned for me to get up and to follow her. "The windows in this place are bulletproof, so don't start freaking out when you see your room."

It was good that she warned me. I entered my room, and the whole wall facing the forest was glass.

"Bulletproof?" I wheezed.

"Bulletproof," she confirmed. "Your bathroom's through there. It has a shower. Mike'll drop some clothes in here while you're in there." She paused at the door as she was leaving. "Do try to get some rest. Everything will look better tomorrow."

"Okay." I didn't know how that was going to be possible without Jacey, but I figured that was a problem for the next day.

Bea left, and I went to go shower. By the time I got out, Mike had left me a couple of pairs of boxers, sweatpants, socks, and a T-shirt on the hope chest at the foot of the bed.

I pulled on a pair of boxers and left the others folded and ready for tomorrow. Then I slid into what must have been some very high thread count sheets.

Still, I couldn't make myself sleep. I tossed and turned, but it was no use. Without Jacey there, the bed felt empty. And that made me replay over and over in my head being torn away from her while bullets were flying.

Sitting up, I finally gave up and started playing with the remote next to the bed. A television popped out of the foot of the bed.

"That works," I mumbled, turning it on and scrolling through to a streaming service.

I ended up watching a cake baking show where they tried to tell the difference between fondant cake and the real object it was created to look like. It was just the kind of mindless TV I needed to take my mind off Jacey. As best I could, anyway.

Morning dawned beautiful and fiery red over the tops of the pine trees after a few hours. I paused the cake baking show to watch.

My heart ached. I wished more than anything I could share this with Jacey.

TOGETHER AGAIN

-Jacey-

The cabin was huge with triangle-shaped windows under the roof line extending to the wraparound deck.

"Wow," I breathed.

"It's nice. It belongs to a senator," Max said. "They're donating it to the joint task force so that we can nail Masterson, the sheik, and a few others. It's all one big trafficking ring, and even when they're competing with each other, they work with each other on occasion as well."

"I suppose it's good to have friends," I muttered.

Max laughed. "No kidding. Ah, here's Bea. She's your new handler–for now. That's all I know. Bea, how's it going?"

"See? You at least know how to deliver a package," the business-dressed blonde woman said.

"Brandon bring one in damaged again?" he sighed.

"If he'd been a pizza, we'd have lost the pepperoni in transit," she lamented.

"Bummer." Max gave me a little push. "This is Jacey. Even managed to stop Ibrahim from taking advantage before handing her over."

Bea nodded. "That's good. Brandon beat his."

"Is Caleb already here?" I interrupted. "Did he get beat up?"

"He's here. He's mostly fine. I'm just complaining," she said. "Come on in. I think he's still watching one of those baking shows. You know, the ones where they make cakes that look like everyday objects?"

"I love that show!" Max exclaimed.

She frowned at him. "No, Max, you can't stay in the big pretty lake home."

He gave a fake pout. "Killjoy. Well, I'll be seeing you around, Jacey! Take good care of each other!" He sauntered back to his car, drove past us to turn around by the large garage, then left with a wave.

I was so agitated I started shifting from foot to foot. "Can I go see Caleb now?"

"Sure. Front door's unlocked," Bea said.

I raced up the wooden stairs and pounded down the deck, making slap-slap sounds with my sandals on the wood, then burst through the door. "Caleb?" I called. "Caleb!"

Two men looked up from playing cards at the dining room table. "You must be Jacey," one of them smiled.

"Forget it, Mike. She's taken," Bea snorted, coming in behind me. "Caleb! Get your butt out here!"

A door in a hallway off to the side that seemed to lead to the bedrooms opened up, and Caleb popped his very bruised head out. His lip was cut, and one eye was swollen shut. "Jacey?"

"Oh my God, Caleb," I gasped. "What happened to your—"

Caleb ran to me and hugged me so hard it knocked the wind out of me. "I didn't know you were coming. I was so scared. I thought you were hurt. I was worried you were dead!"

The one called Mike looked at Bea with a frown. "You didn't tell him she was coming?"

"I thought Brandon had. Shit, I'm sorry," she said, rubbing the back of her neck. "I didn't mean to leave you in the dark. No wonder you weren't sleeping."

"Caleb. Having trouble breathing here," I wheezed.

He loosened his grip just fractionally, but it was enough. "Oh, baby, I missed you. I'm so sorry. Did… did anything happen to you?"

"No, I'm fine. I guess the deal with Ibrahim included him not molesting me, so, I'm just… fine. But you! Look what happened to you! Did Masterson do that?!" I asked.

"Via someone else's fist, but yeah," he replied. He kissed me, then, over and over and all over my face so I couldn't get another word out.

"I think you two are gonna need your bedroom," Mike said. "Like… right about now."

Caleb finally let me go only to grab me by the wrist and drag me to what I assumed was our bedroom.

It wasn't as though we were going to need separate ones, which he demonstrated by shoving down my jeans, tearing open my panties, pulling out his cock, and spearing me against the door.

"Fuuuuck," he groaned as I wrapped my legs around his waist.

It was going to be rough, desperate sex, and I was just fine with that. I was desperate for him, too.

The door rattled on its hinges, leaving no doubt to those outside of what we were doing. We didn't care. I gripped Caleb's hair and tugged while he plunged his big cock into me over and over again, drilling me against the door.

We came together, his hot seed spilling into me just as I reached orgasm.

Then we just stayed like that, panting together.

I brushed a kiss over his swollen eye. "Are you really okay?" I asked him.

"Now I am," he whispered, possessing my mouth with his tongue.

"Bed," I moaned when I felt him hardening again.

He didn't pull out. Instead, Caleb gripped my ass and carried me to the bed, laying us both down with a bounce that made his cock go deeper still.

My eyes rolled back in my head at the tingles that caused throughout my sensitized body.

"You like it when I go deep?" he murmured against my skin, kissing my neck from shoulder to ear.

"Yes," I sighed, holding his head in my hands as he feasted on me like a starving man.

We'd been apart less than two days, and he was still determined to make up for lost time. I didn't mind one bit.

Caleb and I made love for hours. The sun had begun to set in the sky when we finally calmed to just touches and soft kisses. I was going to be so sore in the morning, but still not nearly as sore as him. "I'm worried about all those bruises," I said, playing my fingertips over his chest. "Won't you hurt more tomorrow?"

"Worth it," he replied, twisting strands of my hair around his index finger and then letting them fall in long curls.

I kissed the cut on his lip very gently. "I don't want you to be in pain."

"I'll ask for a frozen steak or a bag of frozen peas or something tomorrow and hold it on the worst parts," Caleb shrugged. "It is what it is, and I wouldn't do anything differently."

"I love you," I said, cupping his cheek.

He took my palm and kissed it then kissed me on the lips. "I love you, too."

We fell asleep that way, tangled up in each other, more hopeful about the future.

———

THE NEXT DAY, when we came out to breakfast, Mike and Ed were smirking.

"Hungry?" Mike teased.

Bea was holding a cup of what smelled like very strong coffee. Her sour expression told me she wasn't a morning person. "You know your bedroom is right next to mine, right?" she complained.

My hand flew to my mouth, and I looked at Caleb. He'd woken me up after a few hours so we could have very loud sex in the middle of the night. "Sorry," I winced.

"Mm-hmm." She yawned. "Well, today is the hand-off to another set of handlers to get you to a new location. I don't know where it is, but it's been fun babysitting you."

"Um… thanks?" I squeaked while Caleb wandered over and got a piece of toast. He buttered it and smeared on some strawberry jam, then handed it to me.

I was hungry, so I bit into it right away.

"They'll be here in about half an hour. I told them you were both going to need clothes," she continued. "Until then, you might as well eat and watch your baking show."

Caleb piled a plate high with bacon and more toast for me. Someone had been thinking ahead, and there was more than enough food for everyone. This was a good thing as Caleb's plate was even more mountainous than my own.

After breakfast, instead of watching the baking show, we played 500 with Mike and Ed. Bea took the opportunity to take a short nap.

Rather soon, there was a knock on the door.

Bea yawned and got up, letting in what looked to be the next handlers. "Welcome," she said.

"Thanks for having us. This place looks great," one of the new handlers said. "Really swanky."

"It is," Mike gushed. "There's a sauna and everything!"

"Nice," one of the other new handlers responded.

"I trust he doesn't need a doctor?" the third handler, a woman, asked.

Bea looked at Caleb. "Nah. He was just slapped around a little. Nothing broken. Doesn't seem to need stitches."

"That's good," the woman said.

Caleb gave them a thumbs-up and slid his arm around my shoulders, kissing me on the temple. "I've got everything I need right here."

The woman laughed. "Well, aren't you two cuter than a puddle of puppies."